THE BILLIONAIRE BRANSON BROTHERS: CARSON

A SECRET SON, SMALL TOWN BILLIONAIRE ROMANCE

LEXI MASTERS

THE BILLIONAIRE BRANSON BROTHERS: CARSON

A SECRET SON, SMALL-TOWN BILLIONAIRE ROMANCE

Lexi Masters

1

NEW IN TOWN – CARSON

The afternoon sun glints off my watch as I step through the door of the quaint diner, the bells above it jingling merrily. I smooth my hand over my crisp suit, glancing around. Checkered floors, chrome accents along the counter, and vintage Coca-Cola ads...it's like stepping back in time. A welcome change of pace from the sleek high-rises and business meetings that occupy my days.

A blonde woman looks up from wiping down a nearby table, cloth in hand. Our eyes meet—hers a striking blue and narrowed slightly. Naomi, according to the name tag pinned neatly to her uniform. I recognize her as the woman I glimpsed through the front window, bustling about with single-minded purpose. That's what drew my attention, and she's the reason I stepped inside.

"Afternoon," I say, giving her a polite smile. She returns a cursory nod, her guard clearly up as she sizes me up. Can't blame her—my tailored suit must look strangely out of place in this cozy establishment.

I make my way to the counter as Naomi resumes her

task, movements efficient and practiced. A woman comfortable in her domain. She finishes up and tosses the rag under the sink before coming over to take my order, ponytail swishing behind her.

Up close, I note little details—the subtle strength in her posture, the determined set of her jaw, the way a few unruly blonde strands frame her face, softening it, and the warmth behind the caution in those intelligent blue eyes. A fascinating contradiction.

"Coffee?" she asks briskly, grabbing a mug.

"Please. Black."

I watch her pour, the rich aroma awakening my senses. As she slides it over, our fingers brush. Unexpected sparks. Her eyebrows lift briefly before she smoothes her expression, but I caught that unguarded flicker of intrigue in her eyes.

"Thank you..." I let my gratitude hang in the air between us, hoping she'll open up.

"Naomi," she says after a beat.

"Naomi," I repeat. "Lovely name." I take a sip, savoring the bold flavor. Through the steam wafting between us, her subtle perfume teases my nose—warm vanilla. "I'm Carson."

She gives a single nod. I try again to engage her. "This is a charming little place. Has it been around long?"

She relaxes slightly, a glint of pride entering her eyes. "My great-grandfather opened it back in nineteen twenty-seven.

"Nineteen twenty-seven?" I let out an impressed whistle. "So, this place is practically part of the town's history."

"It is," she says, a hint of warmth creeping into her tone. "My great-grandad came over from Ireland. Wanted a place for folks to feel at home."

I glance around the cozy space and can easily imagine locals and regulars tucked into the chrome-accented booths or lined up at the counter, sharing a meal. "He'd be proud it's still going strong."

She smiles slightly, but it doesn't reach her eyes. "Doing my best anyway."

I sense there's more she's not saying. Is the diner struggling? Before I can ask, she deftly changes topics.

"I'm guessing you didn't just stop in for the history lesson. What brings you to town?"

"Just passing through." I keep my answer vague. I'm not planning to reveal my real reasons for visiting Branson to anyone just yet. I gesture at my suit. "Clearly, I'm a bit over-dressed for the locale."

"We don't get your type around here often." There's a note of suspicion in her voice. I can't blame her for wondering what I'm after.

I give her my most disarming smile. "I'm certainly glad curiosity led me here, to this charming diner." I lock gazes with her before adding, "And your delightful company."

There it is again, that subtle spark behind her guarded expression, before she busies herself wiping down the counter, ponytail swaying, but the hint of pink in her cheeks gives her away. "Let me know if I can get you anything else," she says quickly, but she doesn't avoid my gaze when she lifts her head. Progress.

"I think just your number, to start," I reply boldly. Then I simply sip my coffee under her surprised stare. Two can play at this intrigue game, and I fully intend to unravel the captivating mystery of this woman.

She eyes me for a long moment, as if trying to solve a complex puzzle. Then the corner of her mouth quirks slightly. "We'll see."

Before I can respond, the bells jingle as a couple enters the diner. Naomi gives me a polite nod then smooths her expression into one of professionalism. "Duty calls."

As she walks over to greet the new customers, I watch her go with growing fascination. What secrets lie behind that subtle armor of hers? I'm more determined than ever to find out. As I covertly study Naomi charming customers at the next booth, I wonder—why *did* I first duck into her diner? A subconscious desire for connection? Was it just her shapely figure catching my eye, or was there more to it than that?

Just then, the bells jingle again as a mother and young daughter enter. The woman's weary expression lifts the instant Naomi greets them.

"Mornin' Clara. Hey there, sweet pea." Naomi goes around the counter to crouch eye level with the pigtailed girl. "Think your usual booth's open, and the pancakes are especially delicious today."

"Can I have them with extra whipped cream?" asks the girl hopefully.

"You betcha, as long as your mom agrees. Be there in two shakes with some menus." Naomi playfully ruffles the girl's hair before straightening. My curiosity deepens, observing this easy rapport she has with locals.

As she makes her way back behind the counter, she catches me watching her friendly exchange. "I've known Clara since we were about this high." Her hand indicates pint-size. "Her brother was friends with my brother growing up."

Ah, there are the community ties I'd expect for a generational establishment. My impulsive stops at New York diners between business deals would never inspire such warmth. Trying to picture myself so intertwined here feels indulgent somehow, and yet... "There's just something so cozy and welcoming about a good diner," I say aloud.

Naomi's expression softens subtly in understanding. "It feels like coming home."

Our eyes connect. In hers, past that lingering wariness stirred by my expensive suit and vague motives, I glimpse what first drew me to duck inside this haven. That rare spark of someone who could welcome a wandering outsider like myself. If I can earn her trust, maybe there are possibilities here I never fathomed.

Our eyes linger, connected by an unlikely but tangible spark. Naomi glances down first, busying herself wiping the already pristine counter.

"So, what brings a wanderer like yourself to our little corner of the world?" She looks back up, tone gently probing. "Are you really just passing through?"

I rub my chin, scrambling for a plausible story. "I'm something of an investor," I hedge, then gesture at the vintage surroundings. "With an appreciation for places with charm and history worth preserving."

Naomi scans my sharp suit with renewed scrutiny. "The business type, huh? We don't see many Wall Street big shots out this way."

I give a noncommittal shrug. "I go where opportunity leads, but it's been too long since I've slowed down to enjoy the journey." I lift my mug in toast. "Happy to have found this lovely establishment, where the coffee and company both shine."

I'm rewarded by the faintest blush tinging Naomi's fair cheeks once more. She averts her gaze, absently wiping an already clean section of countertop. My curiosity surges at what thoughts might lurk behind that inscrutable exterior.

"Too bad not all the tourists passing through appreciate

what we have to offer here..." She nods out the window, where two teens gesture aggressively near a bike rack across the street. My instincts tense, ready to intervene, until a patrol car rolls up. False alarm, just youthful mischief. I turn back to Naomi.

"Sorry, you were saying?"

"Oh, just that our strong community ties help us weather most storms out this way, but new visitors don't always respect that. Some local businesses don't either." Her eyes cloud with unspoken history. My earlier thought, wondering if the diner is struggling, resonate anew, but I merely nod, hoping she'll feel comfortable opening up more in time. For now, I sip my coffee slowly, signaling I'm happy to listen without judgement whenever she's ready.

Unexpected laughter from the mother-daughter pair Naomi greeted earlier floats over, breaking the pensive moment. I watch as she goes to them. The little girl giggles joyously at Naomi's animated antics while taking their order. Witnessing her innate warmth with the townsfolk stirs an unexpected pang in my chest. Longing for that easy sense of community? Or for the company of a certain captivating diner owner, who makes outsiders feel welcomed?

I take another slow sip of coffee, turning over Naomi's earlier words. New visitors don't always respect the close bonds here. Has an insensitive newcomer caused trouble for her in the past? The hints of closely guarded hurt I glimpse in Naomi's expression, usually smoothed over so swiftly, raise my curiosity about what difficulties might truly be facing this proud family legacy.

Before I can delicately probe further, the entrance bells jingle, pulling Naomi's attention and mine. A workers' crew on break files in, trading lively banter. The broad-shouldered man bringing up the rear catches my eye with an assessing gaze that makes me sit up straighter.

"Take any open seats, guys. Be right there," Naomi calls warmly to the new pack of patrons.

As the work crew settles noisily into two adjoining booths, Naomi directs her next unobtrusive question my way while scraping crumbs off the countertop.

"Refill?"

I glance down in surprise to find my mug now empty. Have I really lingered here over an hour already? I nod, pushing the mug forward. Naomi keeps her tone light, but her eyes hold a probing glint. My answers seem to be determining whether I stay in whatever good graces I've found so far.

"So if you're just 'passing through,' any idea where your next 'opportunity' might lead after our little corner of the world?" She tops off my mug, her words casually posed, but her sharp eyes closely gauging my reaction. Just what answer is she hoping for? And why does that suddenly feel so vital for me to unlock?

I take a slow sip, weighing my response. She waits, pot of coffee in hand, as the noisy crew settles into their booths behind us.

Casual words dance on my tongue about continuing my endless business travels, but the alluring spark lingering in Naomi's expression makes me reconsider. Does she want me to linger here too? Or am I imagining things? Either way, opportunity clearly *has* knocked by leading me to this welcoming small-town oasis today. Exploring those possibilities seems far wiser than hurrying on to the next impersonal metro if I hadn't already planned to stay a while due to my real purpose for being here.

I set down the mug, holding Naomi's gaze evenly. "I

think your charming little corner of the world warrants me staying put for a bit actually."

Her eyes widen slightly, but she recovers swiftly. "Glad you're enjoying our hospitality. Did you have lodging set up already or...?"

I rub my chin thoughtfully, a wry smile playing. "Any suggestions?"

"Well, there's 'Margie's Bed and Breakfast' just off Main Street," she says slowly. Behind us, the crew laughs loudly at some shared joke. She ignores them, focused on me. "Very quaint, homey feel."

I sense she's testing me, curious if her small-town charm has truly made an impression on this out-of-towner. I could play into those assumptions, but a gentlemanly suite would actually better aid my quiet investigations here.

I meet her eyes. "I'm sure that homegrown spot is delightful, but I booked a suite at the Chateau On The Lake. I prefer the amenities and service of a luxury establishment."

Naomi lifts a surprised brow but nods, clearly filing away this detail. I'm encouraged that she seems genuinely interested in me, though I should probably keep my distance from everyone until I decide how to move forward on the reason for coming here.

As she moves off to finally tend to the boisterous crew, I lean back contentedly on my stool, the rich coffee warming me to my core. An unexpected sense of belonging bridges the New York investor and the sassy small-town waitress today.

2

HARSH REALITY – NAOMI

The coffee pot shakes slightly in my hand as I pour refills for the boisterous construction crew. I keep flashing back to my odd interaction with the dapper stranger at the counter. Carson. The way he studied me so intently with those dark eyes, as if searching for...something. My pulse quickens, and I splash hot liquid onto my hand.

"Ow." I set the pot down hastily, shaking away the sting.

Jenny glances up from wiping the table nearby, her brown ponytail swishing. "Whoa, you okay over there?"

"Yeah, just burnt myself a little." I walk to the sink to run cool water over my pink skin, willing my whirring thoughts to settle, but questions keep swirling about the curious newcomer with the Texan accent and penetrating gaze. Why is someone like him really lingering in our little town? And why do those eyes keep piercing my composure when they catch me off guard?

Jenny crosses her arms, leaning a hip against the counter. "I know that look."

I shut off the tap and grab a towel, avoiding her probing stare. "What look?"

"All moony while you were chatting up Fancy Suit back there." Jenny hitches her chin at where Carson sat for ages. "What's his story anyway? Some hotshot passing through?"

Heat crawls up my neck that has nothing to do with the burn. "I have no idea, and I was just being friendly."

Jenny lifts one dubious brow. "Uh huh. Is that why you've checked the door four times since Prince Charming left?"

I whip my head up instinctively yet again before I can catch myself. Jenny laughs while I fight embarrassment.

"I think His Royal Highness made quite the first impression on our sassy Naomi." Jenny winks.

The entrance bells save me, clanging loud enough to halt conversation, but I can't focus on the new customers. Why *does* Carson's unexpected visit leave me so off kilter? And why do I desperately hope he'll reappear, as unlikely as that seems for a wanderer staying at the fancy Chateau On The Lake?

Before I can contemplate further, the daily mail pouch thumps heavily onto the counter. My heart sinks, smile fading. Please no more bad news... I reflexively grab the familiar bank envelope first. My hands shake slightly, tearing open the seal. This has to be good news. It just has to be. Surely, the loan officer approved my request for another extension...

My stomach drops reading the mercilessly bold header: Final Notice.

The letter blurs before me. Same damning message. Accounts still behind despite countless small sacrifices to afford bare minimum vendor payments lately. All my determined promises to keep this diner—my family's legacy and the town's special community hub—alive and thriving on my watch seem increasingly hollow.

Crushing defeat threatens to drown me. Then Jenny touches my shoulder gently. Concern fills her eyes behind her friendly smile. My breaths come a little easier. If people like her still believe in this place, how can I give up hope yet? My great-grandfather's cherished establishment has survived world wars and depression years before. This crisis will pass too. I just need the right idea before the bank's patience runs out.

Jenny squeezes my arm comfortingly, clearly having realized the notice means my extension wasn't approved. "Why don't you take fifteen and clear your head a bit? I can hold down the fort."

The kind offer cracks my composure. I manage a swift nod before ducking into the back room just as the prickling tears spill over. Alone among shelves of supplies symbolizing both pride and burden now, my fingers curl into fists. I dash the drops away fiercely. No time for feeling sorry over troubles I swore to conquer to preserve this family treasure.

I just have to keep believing that somehow, things will work out. My great-grandfather brought laughter and community to this town decades ago. I can't fail them all now.

Squaring my shoulders, I smooth my uniform and hair before stepping out with a brighter smile. Chin high, I get back to work, determined to carry my duties—and this establishment—forward another day.

The familiar motions soothe me, broken only by my lingering thoughts occasionally drifting back to the dark-eyed stranger, who might reappear someday, but I have no time for distractions now.

I have a business to save.

I top off Maggie's coffee with a smile, listening as she animatedly shares her latest fishing exploits. Her tales always brighten my day, even when my thoughts threaten to spiral darkly.

As Maggie leaves, satisfied with our chat, I notice her tip dwarfs what most patrons bothered leaving today. Bless her generous soul. My fingers curl around the bills, both grateful and gloomy. Kind gestures won't fund operations much longer if I can't boost revenue soon though.

I glance up, catching Jenny watching me pocket the meager earnings. I straighten swiftly, grabbing a new pot, but her understanding look makes my throat tighten unexpectedly. She and our loyal regulars feel like family. If I can't keep the doors open...

"Table eight's trying to get your attention," she says quietly, gesturing.

I refocus on serving mode, pushing aside money woes I can't fix this instant anyway. Time enough for fretting after hours spent finalizing orders and totals, but the minutes still crawl by, every friendly patron's lingering chat both comforting and indefinitely postponing when I'll have to face the harsh books again.

As Mabel and her knitting circle pay their tab and amble out, Jenny starts wiping down empty tables while humming softly to herself. I envy her positivity sometimes. My shoulders knot tighter every time the entrance bells jingle, torn between desperately needing more customers and dreading facing my problems once closing nears.

When a few teenage boys shuffle in and pick a booth, Jenny glances my way in silent query. I shake off my bleak mood the best I can and paste on a welcoming smile. Just more vital patrons to provide for right now.

I grab menus and head over, wincing internally a little at their boisterous laughter. Definitely not big tippers, but their antics still remind me of my own brother back in high school. Nostalgia and melancholy war inside me. Will the next generation get to enjoy cold sodas and hot burgers here too if I fail?

As I take orders, laughter erupts again, gratingly loud at the boys' crude joke, but my thoughts have already drifted. If I could lure steadier patrons in, boost community ties again like the old days...make this not just a beloved institution but also a smart business...

My gaze goes unseeing out the windows. If only an investor might help modernize without tarnishing this sanctuary's charm...someone open-minded but also pragmatic in saving endangered spaces so rich in history...

You're thinking about Carson again.

Heat flushes my cheeks even as I internally scold myself. A worldly businessman stopping in randomly hardly signals viable partnership potential.

And yet...when our eyes met earlier, his interest felt oddly sincere. Those dark irises piercing me with unexpected connection that whispered maybe, somehow, he might truly understand keeping cherished places like this alive if given the chance.

A loud thump jolts me back to the present. One of the boys has dropped a menu, smirking cockily when I glance his way at the disruption. My shoulders tighten. Reckless youth making noise hardly helps the survival odds of places like this for future generations.

As I finish up with the giggly group, my gaze finds Jenny wiping another table while sneakily watching me again. Concern etches faint lines along her smiling eyes now. My oldest friend and most stalwart ally through every struggle here the past decade. Just the sight of her eases my anxiety a bit.

Maybe alone I'd crumble beneath these worries trying to smother family legacy and personal dreams alike under their relentless weight, but with loyal support like Jenny's, somehow, we'll weather this storm the same way we always do—together.

The evening drags on, my smile growing more forced and footsteps heavier. Closing time creeps closer, when I'll have to face the harsh reality of the diner's dire straits laid out in unforgiving black and white on spreadsheets and orders waiting.

I glance up as the entrance bells jingle, surprised to find Sheriff Bigsby ambling in, Stetson in hand. His amiable face creases into a smile beneath his impressive mustache.

"'Evening, Naomi. Got time for a quick cuppa joe before shutting her down tonight?"

I manage a wan but grateful smile. "For you? Always." I pour him his usual hearty mug. "How're things looking out there, Sheriff?"

He accepts it with a pleased sigh. "Oh, quiet enough, I suppose. Heard there was some ruckus near the Chateau yesterday." My pulse quickens inexplicably. "Turned out to be just a couple rowdy tourists moving along."

I nod politely, hoping no telltale signs of my piqued curiosity at mention of Carson's lodgings show. Thankfully, the sheriff redirects the conversation himself.

"Say, Millie was just telling me yesterday she hoped you'd be entering your family's award-winning pie recipe in the Founder's Fair contest next month." He winks over his coffee mug. "Folks do love that cinnamon apple even more than Millie's."

I manage a thin laugh. If only delectable sweets could fix monetary woes. Although perhaps some extra income from contest winnings might help trim debts, and nothing brings the community together like our annual celebration of Branson's roots.

I tuck that spark of inspiration away to revisit later tonight during my fretful figures analysis. For now, I simply enjoy a few minutes of easy rapport with our genial sheriff, a reassuring pillar of our little world here. All too soon though, he drains his last warming drops and pushes up from the counter with a grateful tip of his hat.

"Much obliged for the brew, Naomi. You take care now."

"You as well, Sheriff. Stay safe out there." I watch him amble out, heavy doors swinging slowly shut in his wake. My shoulders sag once more without a visitor here to put on brave fronts for now.

Jenny joins me behind the counter, tossing her rag into a bin. "About that time, hmm?" Her gentle tone matches the understanding in her eyes. My throat tightens. I simply nod.

Together, in companionable silence, we finish closing tasks as I mentally gird myself for facing the numbers awaiting me. The last chairs get wiped and stacked, and final crumbs swept away. With no more busywork left to delay the inevitable, Jenny gives my shoulder a comforting squeeze.

"I'll lock up tonight. You go on and take care of what you need to." Her confidence in me loosens the choking tension in my chest, if only slightly

Somehow, no matter how harsh realities might seem once I sit down to reckon overdue accounts and desperate shortfalls, having someone Jenny believing I'll churn up an answer makes even fathomless problems feel surmountable.

I can conquer this. I must, for the sake of everything

family and familiar counting on me to navigate these treach-
erous financial straits back into calmer fiscal waters again. I
head wearily into the office. Time to chart an escape course
for this foundering ship before she sinks for good.

3

BOLD PROPOSITION – CARSON

I straighten my tie as I stride toward the diner, eagerness putting a pep in my step this morning. Thoughts of Naomi and her charming little establishment had me awake early, contemplating new ideas. Perhaps my business instincts could truly help modernize her struggling family treasure and engage more of the townspeople to invest in its legacy. Assuming I haven't misread the situation. She could be making a killing already and not need any help, but I don't think that's the case.

As I enter, the bell chimes above me. I spot Naomi behind the counter, ponytail swishing as she pours coffee for an elderly couple. Her eyes meet mine briefly in surprise as I take the same seat at the counter. Was that a glimmer of gladness flashing across her features before it vanished?

"Back again, I see," Naomi remarks, not unkindly, as she approaches for my order.

I give her my most winsome smile. "It's not just the exemplary coffee calling me here."

Her cheeks tinge faintly at the implied compliment before she turns brisk again. "So, what'll it be today?"

I lean back, considering her thoughtfully. Time to take a bold risk on impulse again, just as when I first ducked in on a whim a couple of days ago seeking distraction, only to somehow find captivating new opportunity instead. "Actually, I have a business proposal for you today."

Naomi lifts one eyebrow, curiosity glinting through her wariness now. "What kind of proposal?"

I lace my fingers together. "It's clear even in the short time I've been here that your family's diner means everything to Branson, but the hard truth is, struggling establishments rarely survive on nostalgia alone these days."

Her expression clouds, pride bristling. I rush on gently. "Which would be such a loss for this community, but with the right strategy for revamping menu, service model, and branding,—I believe a partnership could strengthen everything your grandfather worked so hard to build." I meet her stormy eyes. "I'd like to invest in this place. Help me modernize without losing all that history and charm. Together, we could create something truly special."

Naomi stares, lips parted, before finding her voice. "You...you want to invest in my family's diner?" She sounds cautiously intrigued but still hesitant.

I press my advantage. "I have experience reinvigorating beloved spaces on the brink. You know in your heart, change is needed here. I can provide that, plus capital, without sacrificing what makes this place uniquely special." I reach to lay my hand over hers. "I want to help save this community touchstone and make your family proud again. What do you say?"

Naomi looks down at my hopeful grasp, conflict playing across her face. She slips her hand away. I feel her withdrawing and rush to persuade her more, but she holds up a staying palm.

"I know you mean well..." She sighs, absently swiping the already-clean counter. "And while your offer's generous..." She shakes her head slowly, looking up with resolve burning in those ocean eyes now. "My grandfather poured his whole heart and life into building something special here. I won't fail his memory or legacy by handing those reins over to some investor." She meets my gaze levelly. "This diner will see better days soon enough, but I have to be the one to make that happen."

I sit back, exhaling in frustrated admiration even as I scramble to re-strategize. Naomi epitomizes captivating moxie and conviction, but how to convince her our collaboration could be exactly what her family's legacy needs? I just have to keep chipping at that stubborn resistance, and charming my way closer to her guarded heart holds its own attractions now too.

"My offer stands if you reconsider." I smooth my tone, hoping to lighten the sudden tension. "I do understand pride in independence, believe me. Either way, I still look forward to enjoying your hospitality when I drop in."

Some of the defensiveness fades from her taut expression. "As long as you keep appreciating the heart in this place, you'll always be welcome here." A ghost of a grin teases her lips now too. "Even if you are some hotshot outsider."

I chuckle at the accurate jab, relief sinking in as we reconnect. I struck out proposing a buyout today, but time still remains for a partnership here. With a woman as spirited and captivating as Naomi guarding the realm, I anticipate savoring every moment spent working toward thawing her resistance.

An idea strikes, and before I can overthink, I decide to press my luck while the tension has thawed. "You know, I had an idea. Perhaps you'd allow me to properly apologize for coming on so strong just now with all this business talk." I give Naomi a hopeful look. "Would you be free to have dinner with me tomorrow evening?"

Naomi blinks, looking caught off-guard. "Oh, well..." She glances away as if considering, with that alluring hint of pink gracing her fair cheeks again. As she wavers, I play my strongest card with an entreating smile.

"Have you been to the Chateau Grille by any chance?"

Her gaze darts back to mine, lit with surprise and intrigue. "I've heard good things but never gone myself. It's so fancy..."

I nod encouragingly. "Exactly. They just hired a new Parisian chef, and the views of the lake are stunning." I catch and hold her gaze meaningfully. "The perfect way for me to apologize for my clumsy proposition earlier with a special night, if you'll allow me the honor?"

A smile tugs at those softly parted lips now. "If it means that much to you..." She attempts nonchalance, but her eyes sparkle, giving her away. "I suppose one evening couldn't hurt."

Triumph and deeper affection surge in me alike. We discuss logistics briefly, but details blur in my rush of victory. The bigger war is far from won yet on potential investment, but coaxing guarded Naomi to my side, even for a single special dinner date, feels like a pivotal triumph, nonetheless.

As I stroll out shortly after, she graces me with a gentler parting smile than usual. I read shy excitement in her eyes at the extravagance planned for tomorrow night. Though what truly has me eager is simply more time getting lost in her lively spirit over fine wine without distractions.

Wooing local royalty like the fiery diner owner promises

intriguing challenges different from my usual wealthy dates, and the spark glowing brighter between us now warms this gambling heart to the work ahead. I continue wandering downtown, nodding politely to shopkeepers while marveling at the charming small-town vibes permeating everything. Passersby wave merrily whether they recognize me or not. Quite a change of pace from the aloof metro denizens back home.

As I pause to admire flowers blooming outside a bakery, a voice calls out behind me.

"Morning, stranger."

I turn to see an athletic-looking man about my age holding the door for a pretty brunette joining him. The cowboy hat and well-worn boots label him a local. Hopefully a friendly one, unlike the occasional suspicious glances I still notice around town since arriving to quietly investigate my ties to this region.

"Sorry to startle you," says the woman warmly. "I'm Fallon, and this is my husband, Wyatt."

I return her smile. "Carson. Pleasure to meet you both." Up this close, timeworn creases around Wyatt's eyes suggest he smiles often, but sharp intelligence lurks in that steady gaze too.

"New to town?" asks Wyatt in his easy drawl.

I nod. "Still getting my bearings."

Fallon gestures behind her with a grin. "We'll happily offer recommendations if you ever need local perspectives."

"We'll let you get on with your day, but nice chatting!" Wyatt touches the brim of his hat cordially. The couple waves before strolling on, hand in hand.

I watch them go, considering the luck of this encounter. If I can befriend more prominent names during my extended spontaneous visit here, perhaps the family history answers I seek will unravel far smoother than expected...

Buoyed by such auspicious introductions already, I continue my wandering with a fresh spring in my step, pausing to peek in various homey shops. This cheerful riverside community continues delighting me with its unexpected treasures, and somehow, they keep tying back to the feisty diner owner occupying far too many of my wandering thoughts lately too.

4

OVERHEARD SECRETS – NAOMI

I pour coffee on autopilot, barely registering familiar faces drifting in and out of the diner. My thoughts race with closer anxiety the longer Carson occupies them. His dinner invitation sparks intrigue that wars with practicality. Now getting ready to actually step into some fairy tale evening at his side has doubts swarming. Mostly whether I can match wits with someone so at ease in his polished sphere. Or hazard my heart next to his despite the risky spark between us I still can't reason away.

The entrance bell dings, and I glance up to find Fallon breezing inside, glowing despite the early hour. My frazzled state must show. She frowns playfully, taking a stool. "Whoa. Bad batch of bacon this morning?" When I just toy with the coffee pot absently, she presses on. "Come on, what's going on in that head of yours?"

I hesitate, then decide to confide in a hushed tone, aware of the other patrons. "I've got a date with Carson tonight. He just showed up out of the blue yesterday, made an offer on the diner, and then asked me out to dinner at Chateau Grille at Chateau On The Lake Resort."

Fallon's eyes widen, a spoonful of sugar pausing mid-air. "Hold up, the same Carson who just arrived in town a few days ago? And he wants to buy the diner? That's... a lot."

I nod, stirring my coffee aimlessly. "Exactly. It's all so sudden, and this dinner is not exactly at our usual hangouts. I'm out of my depth here."

She sets down her spoon, her expression thoughtful. "This could be something different and exciting. Aren't you a bit curious about him? About why he's interested in the diner... and maybe you?"

A shiver runs down my spine at the thought. "Curious, yes, but also wary. I mean, what are the odds? A handsome stranger strolls into town and suddenly wants to buy my diner, and take me out to the fanciest place around? It sounds like a plot from a romance novel."

Fallon chuckles. "Life can be stranger than fiction sometimes. Maybe you should go to find out his story. You never know. It might be worth the risk."

Her words linger in my mind as I weigh my options. Carson is an enigma, and despite my reservations, I can't deny the pull of intrigue he's awakened in me. The rest of the morning passes in a blur of clinking dishes and murmured conversations. Fallon's words echo in my head, mingling with my own doubts and the all-too-frequent glances at the door, half-expecting, half-dreading to see Carson walk in.

By the time I flip the 'Closed' sign and lock the diner's front door, my decision is made. I'm going. Nervous energy courses through me as I head home to get ready. Each step feels like a commitment, each thought a question mark.

At home, I stand in front of my closet, feeling out of place in my own skin. What do you wear to a dinner with a man who might be buying your livelihood out from under you? I settle on a dress that's comfortable yet flattering, hoping it strikes the right balance between casual and trying too hard.

Carson arrives precisely on time, his car purring to a stop outside my house. He's dressed in a way that's effortlessly stylish, yet not overbearing. As I slide into the passenger seat, our eyes meet and something unspoken passes between us.

The evening air is crisp as Carson's car weaves through the streets toward the Chateau. Inside, the soft hum of the engine is a soothing backdrop to our tentative small talk.

"So, Naomi," he begins, his voice as smooth as the leather seats we're nestled in, "what's your favorite thing about running the diner?"

I smile, feeling the warmth of the question. "The people, definitely. There's something about being part of their daily routine, a witness to their lives."

He nods, genuinely interested. "I can see that. It's like you're a part of the community's fabric."

The conversation flows as we arrive at the Chateau Grille, a stunning vista of Table Rock Lake greeting us through the expansive windows. The ambiance is a blend of elegance and comfort, making me feel both out of my element and strangely at ease.

At our table, Carson's charm is effortless. Over seared scallops and perfectly paired wine, our conversation flows easily. "Paris just has this vibrant energy—foods and smells and sounds enveloping you strolling cobbled side streets, but the people are the real heart." Carson's eyes take on a faraway glint. "At this tiny hole-in-the-wall I found in Montmartre, owner Monsieur Claude greeting every patron like his own family...his coq au vin still haunts my dreams."

"Mmm, I can practically taste it just from your divine

description alone." I lay my chin on my palm, soaking up more glimpses into his world-roaming adventures.

Carson leans forward, his voice dropping lower. "Perhaps someday I can properly introduce your lovely palate to Monsieur Claude's culinary talents."

My own smile grows coy. "Perhaps so. If your charm persuades me." Under the table my shoe brushes his leg, emboldening me.

A new heat smolders in Carson's gaze now too. We allow charged silence to stretch, only the candle between us flickering.

Eventually I redirect before losing all decorum. "So does relentless ambition ever pause long enough to enjoy the fruits of such success?"

Carson considers my question, absently swirling his wine before meeting my curious eyes. "I used to be constantly chasing the next horizon, never lingering to appreciate where I was, but something in your little corner of the world has given me pause."

His hand reaches to graze mine meaningfully, and this time, I allow my fingers to tangle with his. The rare vulnerable candor behind Carson's suave assurance entrances me. What a gift that my beloved community touched this wandering soul so singularly too.

As dinner winds down, I find myself caught in the gravity of his gaze, the depth there something I hadn't anticipated finding tonight.

"We should walk," he says, a playful challenge in his eyes.

Outside, the night embraces us. The path around the lake is lit by soft lights, casting our shadows on the paved walkway. Our conversation takes a more personal turn, each revelation a thread weaving a stronger connection between us.

We stop at a secluded spot, the lake's surface a mirror to the star-studded sky. He turns to me, his eyes reflecting the moonlight, and in that moment, everything else fades away.

We stop at the secluded spot, the lake's surface mirroring the star-studded sky above us. Carson turns to me, his eyes twin moons catching the ethereal light as the laughter drifting from the distant restaurant fades away.

It's just us now alone together with this natural splendor. The subtle spice of his cologne teases my senses again with him standing so near now. Our world narrows only to this little realm apart from everything else.

Carson's fingers graze my jawline, tilting up my chin . "What magic did I ever do to deserve crossing paths with someone as captivating as you?"

His words send delicious tremors through me. I should step back, make polite excuses, and save us both from reckless desires not meant for me, and yet...I can't pull away from the warmth of his touch or presence.

"Carson..." The sound comes as the softest exhalation between us.

His eyes search mine with unspoken questions as he slowly leans closer. My lashes flutter shut just as our lips meet in a kiss unlike any before. Soft yet firm, imbued with tangling hopes and shared longing too long denied us both by past hurts and habits.

My fingers curl into his lapels, breath quickening as we share this timeless, perfect moment here together where nothing else matters beyond us.

We reluctantly pull apart, breathless with pounding hearts yet somehow more at peace than ever before too. As if tasting the first nourishing drops after endless lifetimes spent parched for that perfect kiss.

Carson's thumb grazes my cheek as I worry suddenly how easily my smile could shatter all over again after previous futile attempts at love too soon turned my heart so wary, but rather than playful sweet nothings I brace against, he echoes my deeper concerns intimately too through the way he holds my face so tenderly between hands.

"I know you have your reasons for guarding yourself so carefully, but I swear to you here and now that I will never take lightly you giving me this chance."

His earnest words rush to melt my lingering resistance. Because despite all logic telling me to flee before abandonment bruises my battered spirit again, perhaps I can be brave.

Feeling vulnerable yet strangely fearless too, I loop my arms around Carson's neck to draw him to me again. I gently guide his mouth back to mine in answer, allowing tentative joy to drown out old griefs' dire warnings. Kissing Carson feels like coming home.

After blissful moments alone together under the stars, we reluctantly resume our lakeside stroll back toward the glowing hotel in the distance. A new energy hums between us now, hands clasped together with secrets shared and promises made without need for words.

It feels like we're heading toward something more serious and intense. Spending the night with Carson remains an unwise notion still, however right it felt kissing beneath the moonlight forgetting the world. Yet as we near the ornate lobby doors, the possibility whisks through me— what if he *should* request my company a while longer in his suite upstairs? Would rekindling our private magic together behind closed doors really be so reckless after such a profound connection?

My troubled thoughts churn as Carson escorts me toward the ladies' lounge. "Meet you back shortly," he murmurs, grazing a thumb across my knuckles that sets my skin aflame before walking away.

My reflection in the resplendent room startles me—lips swollen from ardent kisses, and eyes glassy with new secrets. Temptation rises to indulge reckless desires out of character for prudent me, but perhaps this remarkable man merits bending rigid rules.

I smooth my dress, calming racing thoughts with deep breaths. Before overanalyzing further, it's best to return to Carson and let this magical evening unfold however it will.

As I return, ready to face whatever the night holds, I pause. Carson's voice, low and serious, drifts to me from a secluded corner. I have one foot crossing the threshold back to the lobby when Carson's unmistakable voice catches my ear. I still, glimpsing him standing slightly apart, phone cradled intimately against his shoulder.

"Yes, the first acquisitions are nearly complete on this end..." His arm gestures broadly, blazer falling back to reveal an expensive watch glinting even from here. My brows furrow. Acquisitions of what nature exactly?

Eavesdropping warrants shame, but something about Carson's posture radiates shifts from the tender vulnerability by the lake back to cool confidence dealing in dizzying sums far beyond my small-town scope. I strain to listen more closely.

"Yes, the investment is significant," he says, unaware of my proximity. "The diner is just the first step. We'll revitalize the whole area."

The words strike me like a physical blow. Investment?

The diner? My heart races, a blend of confusion and betrayal swirling inside.

I return to the table, my composure barely holding. Carson soon rejoins me, his smile faltering at my changed demeanor.

"I need to go," I say, my mind a whirlwind of doubts and suspicions.

"Is everything all right, Naomi?" His concern seems genuine, but the trust that had been building between us is shaky after hearing his conversation.

"I... I just need some time to think," I say, my mind reeling. I turn and walk away, each step heavy with the weight of unanswered questions.

What are his true intentions? Is this all just a strategic move for some business venture? And where do I fit into this picture? The questions haunt me as I drive home, the echoes of our laughter now distant memories in the face of this unexpected revelation, and the questions it has stirred.

5

COVERT MOVES – CARSON

In the solitude of my hotel room, the night stretches out like an unending road. I'm adrift in a sea of thought, the events of the evening replaying in my mind. The smooth surface of the whiskey glass in my hand is a cold comfort as I try to piece together the puzzle of Naomi's sudden departure.

The room's silence is shattered by the shrill ring of my phone. It's Ellen, my step-grandmother, her timing as impeccable as ever. I brace myself for her inquisitive nature, a trait that's both endearing and intrusive.

"Carson, dear, you sound tense. Is everything all right?" Ellen's voice is a mix of concern and curiosity.

I hesitate before deciding to confide in her. "I had dinner with someone tonight. It was going well, but then she left abruptly. I can't figure out why."

Ellen tsks sympathetically. "These things are never simple, are they? Maybe she's just not the right one."

I find myself defending Naomi, even though I'm still grappling with my own confusion. "It's not that. There's something compelling about her. I just can't put my finger on it."

"Well, dear, sometimes the heart knows before the mind does. Be patient," she says, her voice softening.

We talk a little more, Ellen offering her usual mix of wisdom and gentle probing. By the time I hang up, I feel a renewed sense of determination. I need answers, and I need them now. I set down the phone, Ellen's words echoing in my mind. Her advice, though well-intentioned, does little to quell the storm of questions raging inside me.

I move to the window, the lake outside a dark expanse under the moonlit sky. Naomi's face haunts my thoughts— her smile, the way her eyes lit up in conversation, and then that sudden, inexplicable shift. What caused her to flee from what felt like a genuine connection?

The whiskey burns as it goes down, each sip a futile attempt to wash away the confusion. My mind churns, replaying our conversations, searching for missed signals, or hidden meanings, but the answers remain just out of reach, obscured by the shadows of doubt and uncertainty.

Eventually, I sink into bed, the sheets cool against my skin. Sleep, when it comes, is fitful and haunted by dreams, where Naomi's voice is just a whisper in the wind, always slipping away.

THE MORNING LIGHT brings no clarity, only a deepened sense of purpose. Dressed and ready, I head out to a secluded part of a local park, a place away from curious eyes. Kane, my private investigator, is already there, his presence almost blending into the early morning mist.

"Kane." I nod to him, my voice low.

He turns, his face all business. "Carson. What's the situation?"

"I need information on someone. Naomi Ambrose. She's connected to this diner in town and possibly to the Whitmores. I can't shake the feeling there's more to her story," I say, my words measured.

Kane nods, jotting down notes. "Got it. Anything specific you're looking for?"

"Anything that might explain her sudden change of behavior last night, and her connection to the Whitmores," I sat, a sense of urgency underlying my words.

Kane's eyes narrow thoughtfully. "I'll see what I can dig up. Give me a couple of days."

As we wrap up, movement catches my eye. Fallon, the woman who greeted me the other day, is passing by on a morning walk. Her gaze lingers on me, suspicion etched in her features. Our eyes meet for a moment, a silent exchange that speaks volumes. She moves on without a word, leaving a trail of unanswered questions in her wake.

Kane follows my gaze. "Friend of yours?"

I shake my head. "Complication."

He grunts, understanding. "I'll get you what you need, Carson. You'll have your answers."

With a final nod, he disappears into the park, leaving me alone with my thoughts. Fallon's wary look adds another layer to the mystery. What does Naomi think of me? What has she told her friends about the diner offer? Has she mentioned it? Was that why Fallon gave me a cool look, or was it because I was meeting with a local investigator?

The questions multiply, each one a thread in a tangled web I'm determined to unravel. My mind is racing with possibilities. — With Kane's departure, the park resumes its tranquil morning routine, but my mind is far from peaceful.

I find myself pacing the path, each step an effort to make sense of the situation. Naomi's reaction at dinner wasn't just a casual retreat. It felt like a flight from something deeper, something hidden, and now, with Fallon's suspicious glance, it's clear there's a web of connections I've yet to uncover.

I spend the rest of the morning in my room at the Chateau, a prisoner of my own thoughts. The scenic view from my window, once a source of calm, now feels like a mocking reminder of the distance between me and the answers I seek. My laptop is open, a blank document staring back at me, but the words don't come. The only story that matters now is the one unfolding in real life, and I'm a character without a script.

Lunchtime comes and goes, the usual pangs of hunger absent in the wake of my preoccupation. I make a few calls, touching base with contacts who might offer insights or leads. Each conversation is a dance around the truth, probing for information without revealing too much of my own hand.

As the afternoon sun begins to dip, I decide on a change of scenery. A walk might clear my head and offer a new perspective. I drive to a parking lot downtown before starting to explore. The streets of Branson are a mosaic of everyday life, a sharp contrast to the turmoil inside me. Families on vacation, couples strolling hand in hand, and the occasional local going about their day—they all seem part of a world from which I'm momentarily disconnected.

I find myself drawn to Naomi's diner. A magnetic pull I can't resist, even though I know it might not be the wisest choice. The "Open" sign flickers to life as I approach, casting a warm glow onto the sidewalk. Stepping inside feels like entering a different realm, one where every detail—from the clatter of dishes to the hum of conversation—is a stark contrast to the silence of my hotel room.

Naomi is there, her presence commanding the space behind the counter. She moves with an effortless grace, a dance of efficiency and warmth, but when her gaze meets mine, there's a guardedness I haven't seen before. It's like looking at a familiar painting that's been subtly altered—recognizable, yet unmistakably different.

She approaches my table with a polite, distant smile. "What can I get for you, Carson?" Her voice is steady, but there's an undercurrent of tension that wasn't there before.

"Just coffee, please, and whatever you recommend for dinner." I try to sound casual, but my own voice betrays a hint of the turmoil churning inside me.

She nods, pouring the coffee with a hand that's steady but lacks its usual warmth. "I'll bring you our special for the night. It's usually well-received."

The diner's ambiance wraps around me, a comforting blanket of normalcy that feels oddly out of place now. The conversations at nearby tables, the sizzle from the kitchen, and even the familiar tunes playing softly in the background all feel like parts of a play in which I'm an unwilling actor.

Naomi returns with my meal, placing it before me with practiced ease. "Enjoy," she says, but the word lacks its usual warmth.

"Naomi," I say, wanting to bridge the gap that has formed between us, "About last night..."

She cuts me off with a polite yet firm tone. "I'm really busy right now. We can maybe talk another time."

Her retreat is a silent rebuke, leaving me to my thoughts and the meal before me. The food is delicious, but it's a meal eaten in solitude despite the bustle around me.

As I eat, I watch her move around the diner, interacting

with customers and staff with a professionalism that's tinged with an undercurrent of something else—something I can't quite put my finger on. There's a story here, a depth of emotion and complexity that's just out of reach.

Finishing my meal, I leave payment on the table, including a generous tip. Standing, I take one last look around the diner and then Naomi, who avoids my gaze. The weight of unanswered questions and unspoken words hangs heavily in the air as I step out into the night.

The drive back to the Chateau is a reflective one, the streets of Branson now quiet and dimly lit. The night's events have added layers to the mystery, deepening the intrigue and the challenge. Naomi, the diner, Fallon's wary glance—they're all pieces of a puzzle I'm determined to solve.

Back in my room, I pour myself a drink, the liquid a small comfort against the backdrop of uncertainty. The lake outside is a dark mirror reflecting the night sky, a silent witness to the thoughts that occupy my mind.

Lying in the dimly lit room, the shadows seem to dance with the rhythm of my thoughts. The image of Naomi, serving me with a reserved demeanor, replays in my mind. Her eyes, once brimming with warmth and curiosity, now hold a guarded distance. The change is as perplexing as it is unsettling.

The silence of the night is broken only by the occasional distant sound from outside. A car passing by and the faint laughter of late-night revelers— are reminders of a world moving forward while I'm stuck in a maze of uncertainty.

I turn over, the sheets cool against my skin, and a stark contrast to the warmth of the diner. The comfort of the bed does little to ease the restlessness of my mind. Naomi's sudden shift, the unspoken words hanging between us, and the mystery —why she withdrew form a complex web I'm yet to untangle.

As the night deepens, my thoughts drift to the investigation. What will Kane uncover? Will it bring clarity, or further complicate matters? The anticipation of new information is both a source of hope and anxiety.

I think of the diner, its walls holding stories and secrets. Naomi is more than just a part of it. She seems to be its very soul. Her connection to the place and to the people who come and go, is profound and something I can't quite grasp but desperately want to understand.

The hours pass, each one a slow march toward dawn. When sleep finally claims me, it's a shallow, uneasy slumber, filled with dreams where faces and voices blend into a tapestry of confusion and longing.

The morning light creeps in, casting a soft glow across the room. I wake up feeling no more enlightened than the night before, the puzzle pieces still scattered and elusive. Today, I resolve, will be a day of seeking answers, of delving deeper into the mystery that Naomi and the diner have become. The journey to understanding is just beginning, and I'm determined to follow it wherever it leads.

6

FRIENDLY WARNING – NAOMI

The diner usually has a cozy ambiance that puts me at ease. Today, however, my mind is anything but calm. I'm pouring coffee when Fallon walks in, her stride purposeful, eyes alight with the kind of news that can't wait.

"Morning, Naomi," she says, sliding onto a stool at the counter. "Guess who I saw in the park today, looking all cloak-and-dagger?"

I hand her a mug of coffee, curiosity piqued. "Who?"

"Carson," she says, leaning closer. "And he wasn't alone. He was with Kane Morgan—you know, the local P.I. It looked pretty intense."

Kane Morgan, a name that's well-known in town for his discreet but effective investigative services. My heart skips a beat. "Kane? What were they doing?"

Fallon shrugs, her expression serious. "Couldn't tell, but it didn't look like a casual chat. It was all very hush-hush."

The bell above the door jingles, and I glance up to see Kane himself walking in. The sight of him, so soon after Fallon's revelation, feels like more than just a coincidence.

He nods at me, a polite but distant acknowledgment, and chooses a booth by the window.

I take a deep breath, steadying my nerves. "I'll be right back," I tell Fallon and head over to Kane's table.

"Morning, Kane. Coffee?" I ask, trying to sound casual despite the questions racing through my mind.

He looks up, a hint of surprise in his eyes. "Sure, and I'll take the lunch special too."

I pour his coffee, my hands steady despite the turmoil inside. "You're usually not here this time of day. Something special bring you in?"

Kane takes a sip of his coffee, his gaze meeting mine. "Just needed a change of scenery."

I linger for a moment, trying to read his expression. "I heard you were in the park this morning, with Carson Daniels. Everything okay?"

His eyes narrow slightly, a guarded look crossing his face. "Just business. You know how it is. Confidentiality and all that."

I nod, not entirely convinced. "Of course, just small-town curiosity on my part."

Returning to the counter, I share a look with Fallon. Her raised eyebrows mirror my own concerns. The rest of Kane's visit is uneventful, but the seed of suspicion Fallon planted grows with every discreet glance in his direction.

After Kane leaves, Fallon leans in. "So, what do you think? Anything seem off?"

I wipe down the counter, my mind a whirlwind. "I don't know, Fallon, but there's definitely more to Carson than meets the eye."

I take a deep breath, feeling a mix of trepidation and urgency. "Fallon, there's more. The other night, after dinner with Carson, I overheard him talking about investing and revitalizing the area. It sounded serious, like big plans for the town... and the diner."

Fallon's eyes widen, her coffee momentarily forgotten. "Revitalizing? That sounds... ominous. What does it mean for us, for the diner?"

I shrug, the uncertainty weighing heavily on me. "I wish I knew. It's all so vague, but it doesn't feel right. He's hiding something, and now with Kane involved..."

We fall into a contemplative silence, the diner's morning bustle fading into the background. My mind races with possibilities, none of them comforting. Carson's charming facade is starting to crack, revealing a complexity I hadn't anticipated.

Fallon reaches across the counter, her hand resting on mine. "Naomi, be careful. This sounds like it's more than just a simple investment, and Kane being involved? It's all too convenient."

I nod, feeling a surge of gratitude for her concern. "I know. I'll tread carefully, but I need to find out what's going on. This diner is more than just a business to me, it's my life."

I squeeze Fallon's hand, drawing strength from her support. "Thanks, Fallon. I just feel so out of my depth here."

She gives me a reassuring smile. "You're not alone. Wyatt might be able to dig up some information. He's got connections, you know."

The thought of involving Wyatt brings a mix of relief and apprehension. "Would he do that? I don't want to drag him into this mess."

Fallon nods emphatically. "Of course, he will. Wyatt knows how much this place means to you and to all of us. We're like family. We look out for each other."

Her words warm my heart. The sense of community in our small town has always been our strength, and now, more than ever, I realize its value. "I appreciate it, Fallon. Really, I do. I just hope we're not overreacting to a few overheard words and a secretive meeting."

She pours herself another coffee, her gaze thoughtful. "Better to be cautious. We'll help you figure this out."

Our conversation shifts to lighter topics, but the undercurrent of concern remains. The diner fills up with the lunchtime crowd, the familiar faces and chatter offering a semblance of normalcy amidst the brewing storm.

As the day progresses, my mind keeps returning to Carson and Kane. The pieces of the puzzle are scattered, and the more I try to fit them together, the more they elude me. Each ring of the bell above the door has me instinctively looking up, half-expecting to see Carson walk in, but he doesn't.

In the midst of the lunch rush, my distraction gets the better of me. While flipping burgers on the grill, my hand grazes the hot surface. A sharp pain shoots up my arm, and I hiss, pulling back immediately. The sizzle of the burn is a harsh reminder to stay focused.

"Fallon, I need to step out for a bit," I say, trying to keep my voice steady despite the throbbing in my hand.

She rushes over, concern etched on her face. "What happened?"

"Just a small burn. I'll go see Dr. Jennings at the urgent care," I assure her, wrapping a clean cloth around my hand.

"Want me to come with you?".

I shake my head. "No, it's okay. Keep an eye on things here, and I'll be back soon."

The drive to the urgent care is a blur, my mind still reeling from the morning's revelations and now the searing pain in my hand. Dr. Jennings, a familiar face in the community, greets me with a kind smile that belies his professional concern.

"Let's take a look at that burn, Naomi," he says, guiding me to an examination room.

As he treats the burn, his gentle demeanor is a small comfort. "You need to be more careful," he says lightly. "What had you so distracted?"

I ponder telling him about Carson, Kane, and my growing fears for the diner, but I hold back. Dr. Jennings is a good man, but this feels like something I need to handle within my own circle for now.

"Just a lot on my mind, I guess," I reply, forcing a smile.

He finishes bandaging my hand. "Take it easy for a few days, okay? And try to avoid any more distractions in the kitchen."

I thank him and head back to the diner, my hand bandaged but my mind still unsettled. Jenny looks up as I walk in, relief flooding her features.

"All good?" she asks.

I nod, taking my place behind the counter once more. "All good."

The rest of the day passes in a haze of activity, but the incident at the grill and the visit to Dr. Jennings serve as stark reminders of how much I have at stake. The diner, my staff, and our town—are all counting on me to uncover the truth behind Carson's intentions.

I slip into the routine, the familiar tasks helping to anchor my scattered thoughts. Jenny keeps a watchful eye on me, her concern evident. The lunch crowd slowly trickles out, leaving the diner in a quiet lull, a stark contrast to the storm brewing in my mind.

My hand throbs beneath the bandage, a constant

reminder of my momentary lapse. I can't afford any more distractions, not with so much at stake. The diner has always been my safe haven, my source of pride and joy, but now, it feels like the epicenter of an unfolding mystery.

As the afternoon wears on, the bell above the door chimes intermittently, each new customer a brief diversion from my worries. I find myself glancing at the clock more often than necessary, counting down the hours until closing.

Jenny sidles up to me, her expression serious. "You sure you're okay to keep going? I can handle things here."

I manage a smile, grateful for her offer. "I'm fine. It's just a little burn. I've handled worse."

She nods, but her eyes betray her lingering concern. The day finally comes to an end, the 'Closed' sign turning customers away. Jenny helps me clean up, the clatter of dishes and hum of the refrigerator filling the silence.

"You heading straight home?" she asks as we finish.

"Yeah," I say, slipping off my apron. "I think I need a good night's rest."

She gives me a quick hug. "Call me if you need anything, okay?"

I nod, appreciating her unwavering support. "Will do. Thanks, Jenny."

Locking up, the weight of the day settles on my shoulders. The walk to my car is a solitary one, the evening air cool and refreshing. Driving home, the quiet streets of our small town pass by in a blur, each one holding memories, hopes, and now, growing fears.

At home, I find solace in the small rituals of winding down. The gentle hiss of the tea kettle and the soft glow of the living room lamp are comforts in a world that seems increasingly uncertain.

Sitting on the couch with a cup of tea, I'm joined by

Magdalena, my tortoiseshell cat. She jumps up beside me, her warm, compact body a welcome presence. She purrs softly, her rhythmic vibrations a soothing counterpoint to the chaos of my thoughts.

I stroke Magdalena's soft fur, her patchwork of brown, black, and orange a familiar comfort. She nuzzles against my hand, blissfully unaware of the complexities troubling me. In moments like these, I envy her simple, untroubled existence.

The room is quiet, save for the occasional clink of my spoon against the teacup and Magdalena's contented purrs. My mind, however, is anything but quiet. The day's revelations and Fallon's concern swirl together with my own fears and doubts. Carson's intentions, Kane's secretive demeanor, and the future of the diner weigh me down. —Each thought tangles with the next, forming a knot I can't seem to unravel.

I sip my tea, letting the warmth spread through me while trying to find some semblance of peace in the midst of uncertainty. The diner isn't just a business. It's a part of who I am, a cornerstone of this community. The thought of it being caught up in something unknown, potentially harmful, is unsettling.

Magdalena, sensing my unease, nestles closer, her green eyes gazing up at me with feline intuition. In her simple, unspoken way, she offers comfort and companionship, reminding me of the simpler joys in life.

The clock ticks on, marking the passage of time in the quiet room. I set down my empty cup and gently lift Magdalena off my lap. Standing up, I stretch, feeling the weight of the day in my muscles.

As I prepare for bed, my thoughts keep returning to the diner, to Carson, to the unknowns that lie ahead. I need to be cautious, to gather more information before making any decisions. Crawling into bed, Magdalena jumps up to claim her spot at the foot. Her presence is a small, yet significant comfort.

In the darkness, I close my eyes, hoping for a night free of worries, a brief respite from the storm. Tomorrow is a new day, and with it comes the opportunity to seek answers, to protect what's mine. With that thought, I drift into a restless sleep, the events of the day echoing in my dreams.

Despite my fears, and the uncertainties, I dream of Carson. We're kissing again, and when I wake the next morning, my lips are faintly swollen, probably from me biting them while sleeping, but I wish his lips had actually imprinted on mine. I want to explore the attraction to him, but I can't until I understand his intentions.

7

UNSEEN SHADOWS – CARSON

Integrating into the rhythm of Branson's daily life, I find myself increasingly drawn to its quaint charm. The town, with its friendly faces and unhurried pace, is a stark contrast to the cities I've known. Yet, beneath the surface, I sense a shift, a subtle change in the air, especially around the Whitmores.

I encounter Wyatt a couple of times around town. The first time is at the hardware store, the day after my meeting with Kane, and he's as friendly as last time. The next time I see him, two days later at the ice cream parlor, his demeanor has changed. At the hardware store, he was all easygoing charm beneath that cowboy hat, tips offered freely about where best to grab a bite or wet a line in the area. Just a local good ole boy waxing nostalgic about his riverside stomping grounds to a curious newcomer.

But crossing paths with him now outside the ice cream parlor, the wary glint in his eye gives me pause. His jaw sets subtly as I approach, leathered hands braced on lean hips in unconscious authority.

"Afternoon again, Wyatt," I say politely, hoping to

smooth whatever ruffled this one's feathers since our hardware handshakes.

"Carson." He touches the brim of his hat in taciturn greeting. No nostalgic anecdotes emerge about favorite fishing holes today.

I gesture to the colorful parlor interior, aiming for casual distraction. "I've heard Bessie's ice cream is legend around these parts. Any flavor recommendations?"

Wyatt's boot scuffs the curb, thumbs hooked in belt loops. "Naomi's partial to the black raspberry, though Fallon will talk your ear off about peach ginger." Behind Wyatt, a powerfully built man with a closely shorn scalp pauses in passing, exchanging an unreadable look with my reluctant conversation partner.

I clear my throat, sensing sudden alliance against me. "Trying new flavors sounds wise then."

Wyatt nods, jaw subtly tensed. "Finding the right taste often takes some trial and error. It's best to realize you can't force the flavors to be what you want them to be."

His emphasis makes me wonder if we still discuss desserts, but before I parse his intimation, the other man ambles over to clamp a meaty hand on Wyatt's shoulder. He sizes me boldly up and down. "This fella bothering you or just making small talk?" False congeniality barely masks the challenge.

Wyatt's laugh sounds strained as he waves off his companion. "Nah, Raylan, just discussing who in town prefers what sweet treats. Mr. Daniels here was just on his way."

Another Whitmore. I look quickly and then glance away, trying to commit his face to memory. I resist answering Raylan's posturing, instead politely excusing myself from the suddenly tension-filled streets.

"Enjoy your afternoon then..." I nod farewell before turning crisply away, their drilling gazes warming my back until the shop door closes behind me.

Inside, I take steadying breaths before stepping up to peruse the impressive array of pails and cones, churned confections beckoning innocently enough. No further comrades materialize from Naomi's retinue to warn off the outsider among homey establishments clearly treasured as communal touchstones.

By the time I exit, licking a double scoop of vanilla and strawberry, Wyatt and his crony no longer lurk to warn me off, but I'm sure that was their intention. Why though? I offered to invest in her diner, not swindle her.

I need to speak with Naomi about this growing tension with Wyatt and his brother and get her take on how to smooth local ruffled feathers hampering my efforts here. I walk to the diner as I eat the ice cream that melts on my tongue like pure heaven.

The jaunty bells announce my entrance. Naomi isn't up front charming patrons as usual though. I take my familiar seat, assuming she's just busy in back. The perky pony-tailed server, Jenny, bounces over with a menu. "Afternoon, Mr. Daniels. Our specials today are pot pie or meatloaf..."

I tune out the specials, straining to hear Naomi's honeyed voice from the kitchen or office instead, but no tell-tale laughter reaches me over the midday clatter.

Jenny falters, blinking at my distracted silence until I manage an apologetic grin. "Actually, I was hoping to have a quick word with Naomi if she's available? Nothing urgent if she's occupied."

Jenny shakes her head, curls bobbing. "Oh, sorry, hon. Naomi had to pop over to the bank, but she should be back real soon if you want to just hang tight."

My eyebrows rise in surprise. "The bank? Everything okay?"

Again, Jenny shakes away my concern with a dazzling customer service smile that doesn't reach her eyes, which seem full of worry. "Oh, I'm sure everything is fine. Probably just paperwork or something, you know." At my skeptical look, she rushes on. "Now, you sure I can't get you something while you wait?"

I drum the counter edge, an uneasy feeling creeping in. Naomi having to handle bank business abruptly doesn't bode well after the cold shoulders from Wyatt and Raylan earlier. Is there a connection I'm missing?

"Just coffee for now thanks, Jenny."

As Jenny pours coffee, I ponder what exactly inspired Wyatt and his overgrown pitbull Raylan's subtle hostility earlier. They seem determined to dislike me all of a sudden, which is damned inconvenient, considering the Whitmores are the reason I came to Branson.

The entrance bells jingle, pulling me from uneasy thoughts. An older man ambles in, reeking of whiskey sours and stale tobacco. He staggers over to the counter nearby as I'm fishing my wallet out to pay.

Jenny bustles past, greeting him with forced cheer. "Be with you in just a sec, Mr. Jenkins."

"Well, c'mon then, girlie, I ain't got all day," he grouses loudly, rapping the counter with knobby knuckles.

I straighten, annoyance flaring. "Hey, now, that's no way to address the staff here." I keep my tone level but firm. "Mind your manners or take your business elsewhere."

Jenkins turns at the sound of an outsider's voice, rheumy eyes bleary but sharp. "And who might you be?" He looks me up and down contemptuously. "Some hot shot thinkin' yer better'n us locals?"

"No, sir. I just don't believe in being unkind to waiters."

His eyes narrow. "Wait, I know you. You're that investor fella thinksss he can jus' wander into our lil haven and buy up everything."

I sit straighter as nearby diners glance over, Atticus Finch warnings rising in my brain about small town tempers. "I believe we haven't met properly, sir. I'm Carson."

I offer a polite hand that goes ignored as Jenkins sways, bleary eyes narrowing. "Ohhh, I know yer type all righ'! Swannin' roun' here in yer fancy suit, butterin' up Miss Naomi, turnin' her head with big city dreams..."

Heat creeps into my cheeks as patrons murmur. When did my business overtures become such public gossip poison?

Jenkins jabs my shoulder, reeking of stale booze. "This here's a right fine town. No need for outsiders and their 'prospects' stirrin' up trouble!"

The bite in his words raises my hackles, but I merely signal a nervous Jenny for the check as Mr. Jenkins continues his slurred diatribe. My grand plans to help the area are apparently being painted in far different tones around local bars.

In my distraction, I don't even notice Naomi's return until she smoothly escorts the drunk Jenkins outside, but the fresh tension in her body language warns me this issue touches nerves.

I meet her gaze when she returns. Her smile seems strained. "Sorry for the drama." Naomi takes her time before finally slipping onto the stool beside me. Her eyes cloud with unspoken thoughts when she looks my way.

A lull arrives, allowing the heaviness lingering between us space to settle. I turn toward Naomi, keeping my tone gentle. "I feel your withdrawal lately. Have I done something to lose your trust?"

She blinks rapidly, clearly taken aback. "Not exactly. I just got spooked I suppose..." She worries her lip with her teeth. "I overheard part of your conversation about acquiring businesses in the area, and then Fallon told me you were meeting with that investigator fellow, Kane. It seems strange you're be digging into townsfolk's lives. I want to trust you, but I'm not sure I should."

I wince internally, cursing meeting Kane so openly. "You deserve honesty. I did have him look into prominent area families, purely for investment research purposes though." At Naomi's skeptical look, I spread my hands and struggle not to betray any hint that that's true, but not the full truth. "I'd hoped understanding lineages around here better might reveal how I could gain traction for my development plan."

I expect Naomi's expression to shutter again. Instead, sympathy enters her eyes. "So, we both want what's best for this place but end up at odds somehow..." She sighs, shaking her head. "You'll have a tough job ahead of you convincing people to sell or allow investors. We're pretty independent around here, so I doubt you'll convince anyone."

I grasp her hand lightly. "It can be done. I know it. Right now, I'm just focused on convincing you. What we glimpsed together those first days before doubts crept in—" I wait until her gaze meets mine. "—wasn't that worth fighting for? Even if you don't want a business partner, I think we could have something special that's just personal."

Naomi hesitates, turmoil playing across her features once more. I hold my breath, hoping my words convince her. This time, I'm strictly speaking the truth and want to convince her to take a chance on me.

Eventually, she squeezes my hand back gently. "What we

share does feel special somehow. I guess I got alarmed by how fast things started shifting." Regret clouds her eyes. "You were acting a bit sneaky, but I should have just asked you about it directly."

Buoyed, I lift her hand to my lips. "Yes. Please just talk to me if you have doubts or concerns." I hesitate for a moment before asking, "So, where do we go from here?"

A reluctant but true smile emerges. "I suppose it wouldn't hurt to spend more time together." Her smile turns impish. "In fact, why not start reconciling differences over dinner? I'll cook though. Chateau Grille was nice, but I'd prefer to avoid more fancy distractions."

My laughter rings out, relief bubbling over at having a second chance. Maybe she'll never let me invest in the diner, but I'm more interested in being with her than being her business partner. "That sounds perfect."

She smiles. "Great. I'll close the diner at seven, so be at my place by seven-thirty. I live across the street in the Blue-bell Apartments, number four."

I let out a relieved breath. "It's a date."

8

———

UNEXPECTED REVELATION – NAOMI

The aroma of roasted garlic and rosemary fills my kitchen, the familiar scents grounding me as I prepare dinner for Carson. Each chop and stir is methodical, a rhythm that calms my frayed nerves. The table is set modestly yet elegantly, an attempt to bridge the gap between our worlds.

Carson arrives right on time, a bottle of wine in each hand. "This should complement your cooking," he says with a smile that reaches his eyes. "Red or white, since I didn't know what you're making."

"Thank you," I say, taking the wine. "Dinner's almost ready."

He follows me to the kitchen as I set aside the red wine and find the cork in my junk drawer. After I open the white to accompany the chicken, we sit at the table, the initial awkwardness giving way to a comfortable conversation.

As I pour the wine, its rich aroma mingling with the scents of dinner, Carson watches with an appreciative eye. "You've outdone yourself, Naomi. This looks amazing."

I offer a tentative smile, feeling the weight of our previous encounters. "I hope it tastes as good as it looks."

We start with the salad, its crisp freshness a perfect opener. Carson takes a bite, his expression one of genuine enjoyment. "Delicious. You know, I've always believed that a meal cooked with care is the best way to understand someone."

His words, simple yet sincere, ease more tension between us. "Cooking's always been more than just a job for me. It's a way to connect and share a part of myself."

Carson nods, his gaze meeting mine. "I can see that. There's a warmth in your cooking that makes me feel welcome."

Encouraged by his interest, I find myself opening up about my journey with the diner, the recipes passed down through my family, and the joy of seeing customers' satisfied reactions.

As we move on to the main course, a roasted chicken seasoned with herbs and spices that I dashed across the street to start prepping earlier, during a lull at the diner, the conversation flows more freely. Carson shares anecdotes from his travels, the places he's seen, and the food he's tasted. His stories are peppered with humor and insight, painting a picture of a life both adventurous and reflective.

"I never thought I'd find myself so taken with a small town like Branson," he says, cutting into the chicken. "There's something about this place, and the people here, that's genuinely captivating."

I watch him, seeing the man behind the investor, testing the sincerity in his words but finding no reason to doubt it. "Branson has a way of doing that. It gets under your skin, in the best possible way."

We talk about our dreams, our aspirations, and the

paths that led us to this moment. The initial awkwardness fades, replaced by a connection that feels both new and familiar.

Dessert is a simple apple pie, the crust golden and flaky. I brought it home from the diner, since it was left over from the morning baking. Carson's appreciation is evident as he savors each bite. "You know, I came here with plans and big ideas, but sitting here with you, sharing this meal, I realize there's so much more to this town than just business opportunities."

His admission strikes a chord in me. The barriers I'd built around my heart, around the diner, begin to soften. Maybe, just maybe, Carson isn't the threat I feared he was. Surprisingly, I find myself telling him about Mark. "You're not the first outsider who's breezed through, claiming to be a savior."

He frowns. "I never claimed to be that."

I hesitate but slowly nod. "No, I guess you didn't. You offered a solution, but you never oversold it. Mark Baxter was a stranger staying here one summer to write some dreadful book about the existential crises of the the modern generation, or something like that. He talked a lot about it, but I sort of tuned it out."

He's stiff now. "This Mark gave you problems?"

I shrug. "He offered solutions, but first, he swept me off my feet. We had a whirlwind relationship, where I ignored all the red flags. He started talking about me coming back with him when he returned to St. Louis, and he arranged a realtor to come talk to me, so I'd sell the diner despite me having told him no several times already." I meet his gaze. "I realized right then that my diner was far more important than Mark, who wanted to tell me what to do and control my future. It still hurt a little, but I sent him away, and I've avoided getting involved with newcomers, or much of anyone, since."

"Lucky that I'm not trying to get you to sell it then." He gives me a small smile. "I just want to help."

I make a noncommittal sound, still undecided, and we talk of other things. The evening winds down, and he insists on helping with the dishes. Afterward, he drifts toward the door. As Carson stands near the doorknob, there's a reluctance in his movement, and a clear desire to linger.

"Thank you for dinner. It was more than just a meal. It was a glimpse into your world, and I'm grateful for it."

I walk closer to him, feeling a mixture of contentment and uncertainty. "I'm glad you came. Tonight was...nice."

He pauses at the threshold, his gaze holding mine in the soft porch light. "About our first date... I've been wanting to revisit that goodnight kiss ever since."

A smile tugs at my lips, the memory of our first kiss still vivid. Without a word, I step closer, closing the space between us. Our second kiss feels familiar yet charged with a new depth, a confirmation of the connection we'd felt from the start.

Carson's arms wrap around me, pulling me closer, and the world outside the embrace fades away. The kiss is warm, gentle yet passionate, and speaking volumes of the growing bond between us.

As we part, there's a shared understanding, a silent acknowledgment of something blossoming. "That was definitely worth the wait," he says, his voice soft.

I nod, still caught in the moment. "Definitely."

He lingers a moment longer. "I'd like to spend more time with you. To really be a part of this town you love so much."

"The Fall Festival is this weekend," I say, the idea

forming as I speak. "It's the perfect place to experience Branson's community spirit."

A genuine smile lights up his face. "I'd like that. I'll be there."

"It's a date," I confirm, feeling a mixture of excitement and nervousness.

We say our goodnights, and as I watch Carson drive away, I'm cautiously hopeful that he's all he appears to be and more.. The festival will be an opportunity for him to immerse himself in the life of Branson, to understand why this place is so special, and I hope, allow me to see more of the man behind the mogul.

Closing the door behind me, I lean against it, my thoughts a whirlwind. The night with Carson has been a step toward something new and a chance to bridge the gap between our worlds. The kiss, a blend of promise and understanding, lingers in my mind, a sweet reminder of the possibilities that lay ahead.

THE BRANSON FALL FESTIVAL is a tapestry of autumn colors and festive sounds, the air rich with the scents of cinnamon, apples, and pumpkin spice. The town square is abuzz with activity, locals and tourists mingling amidst stalls and games. I'm there with Carson, watching him navigate this slice of small-town Americana.

"You weren't kidding about the pie contest," he says, his eyes wide as we pass the display of prize-winning desserts. I'd planned to enter a pie but never found the time. The competition would have been fierce if I'd managed to find the time, judging by the perfection in the display cases.

I laugh, enjoying his fascination. "It's serious business

here. Mrs. Henderson has been the reigning champ for three years straight."

As we wander, I introduce Carson to various town folks, proud to show him the community that's always been my backbone. He's charming and engaging, his earlier stiffness giving way to a more relaxed demeanor.

We're near the beer tent, sampling the local brews, when Raylan approaches us. He's a rugged, outdoorsy type, with an easygoing manner that belies the keen observation in his eyes.

"Carson, right?" says Raylan, extending a hand, though his gaze remains assessing. "Heard you're new in town. Name's Raylan Whitmore."

Carson takes his hand, a polite smile on his face. "We sort of met outside 'Bessie's'.. I'm getting to know Branson."

Raylan nods as though he's picking up something more than the obvious message of Carson's words, his gaze flicking between us. "I can't fault that, or your name. Carson's a family name for us Whitmores. Our dad was a Carson."

"Is that so? It's a fine name. I've always liked it," says Carson with a small smile. "Good thing, since I hear it every day of my life."

Raylan chuckles. His demeanor is friendly but with an undercurrent of caution. "Enjoy the festival. Branson's a welcoming place. You'll fit right in as long as you accept the town as it is."

As Raylan walks away, I can't help but feel there's more to the exchange than casual small talk. Carson seems unperturbed, but the mention of his name being a family one for the Whitmores sticks with me.

We continue our tour of the festival, laughing and trying our hand at various games. Carson's ease with the townsfolk is impressive. He seems genuinely interested in their lives and stories.

We're still enjoying the lively atmosphere near the beer tent when Mr. Jenkins, clearly inebriated, stumbles toward us. His gait is unsteady, and his eyes fixate on Carson with a mix of recognition and disdain.

"Look who we have here," slurs Jenkins, pointing a finger at Carson. "The big city guy trying to buy up our little Branson."

Carson maintains a calm demeanor. "Evening, Mr. Jenkins. Maybe it's time to call it a night, huh?"

Jenkins ignores the suggestion, stepping closer. "You think you can just come here and charm everyone? We see through you. We don't need your kind changing our ways."

I can see the situation escalating and step in, trying to defuse it. "Mr. Jenkins, let's not cause a scene. Why don't I help you find a seat?"

He shrugs off my attempt, his focus solely on Carson. "You're not fooling me. I've seen your type before, always wanting more, and taking over small towns for your gain."

Carson's patience seems to wane, but he keeps his voice even. "I'm here to be part of the community, sir. I have no intention of 'taking over.'"

The crowd around us starts to take notice, their festive chatter turning into murmurs of curiosity. Jenkins, emboldened by the attention, raises his voice.

"You think you can just waltz in here like you're one of the Whitmores?" he challenges, a wild look in his eyes.

The mention of the Whitmore name in such a heated accusation sends a ripple through the onlookers. I feel a sudden jolt of realization—the resemblance, the name Carson, his murky reasons for being here...it's too much of a coincidence.

The tension around us is unmistakable. Carson looks at me, his expression a mix of surprise and frustration. "Naomi, I..."

The moment is broken by Raylan stepping in, his voice authoritative. "Enough, Jenkins. You're causing a scene. Time to head home."

As Raylan leads Jenkins away, the crowd slowly disperses, but the seed of doubt has been planted. I turn to Carson, my voice tinged with confusion and hurt. "Is it true? Are you...related to the Whitmores?"

Carson hesitates, then slowly nods. "Yes, but it's not what you think."

I take a step back, the realization washing over me in waves of shock and betrayal. He's been here under false pretenses all along. "Why didn't you tell me?"

He reaches out, his voice tinged with urgency. "Please, let me explain. It's complicated."

I fold my arms, struggling to process the information. "Complicated how? You've been here for weeks, and you never mentioned this?"

He exhales, a mixture of resignation and honesty in his eyes. His expression is tinged with a vulnerability I hadn't seen before. "I came to Branson to understand my roots, to see if there's a place for me in the Whitmore family. They don't know about me, and I wasn't sure how they'd welcome me, if at all."

I stare at him, trying to reconcile this revelation with the man I thought I knew. "So, you're...you're a Whitmore, but they don't know you?"

He nods, his eyes not leaving mine. "Yes. My connection to the Whitmores is... complicated. I didn't want to be defined by it. I wanted to see Branson, understand the town my family is so rooted in, on my own terms."

The pieces start falling into place, but they bring more questions than answers. "And the diner? Your interest in it?"

Carson takes a deep breath. "My interest in the diner started as a part of exploring Branson, but it became more than that after meeting you. My feelings for you, and my plans for the diner, are both genuine."

I'm torn, the weight of this confession heavy on my shoulders. "I don't know what to say. This is a lot to take in."

He steps closer, his voice earnest. "I understand this changes things, but I hope it doesn't change how you feel about what's growing between us. I'm still the same person you've gotten to know."

Raylan's intervention with Jenkins, and the festival's joyous noise all seems distant now. The revelation has cast a long shadow over the night, leaving me to navigate a maze of emotions. "I need time," I say finally, my voice steady despite the turmoil inside. "Time to understand all this."

He nods, a mixture of understanding and disappointment in his eyes. "I'll give you all the time you need. Just know, my feelings for you are real."

We part ways, the festive lights of the square now just a blur. Walking back to my car, I feel a profound sense of uncertainty. Carson's revelation has upended everything, leaving me to ponder the future of our relationship and his place in Branson. The night air is crisp, but the questions that swirl around me are far from clear, each step taking me deeper into a web of lies and truth that seem impossible to untangle.

9

REVELATIONS AND RIFTS – CARSON

The diner's "Closed" sign glows softly in the evening darkness, its usual welcoming warmth now a beacon of my anxious wait. Two days of silence from Naomi have left me in a state of unease, each passing hour amplifying my regret and determination to set things right. She agreed to meet me here, but I'm nervous she won't show until I see her walking across the street.

She's walking briskly, her silhouette purposeful as she approaches. She nods to me as she unlocks the diner. The door opens with a familiar jingle, and Naomi steps in, her expression a mix of resolve and apprehension as I follow behind her.

"Naomi, thank you for coming. We need to talk," I say, my voice tinged with urgency.

She doesn't sit, her stance guarded. "Talk? I've had two days of 'talking' in my head. Two days of trying to make sense of your lies."

I wince at her words, the truth in them cutting deep. "I never meant to lie to you, Naomi. I was trying to protect..."

"Protect what, exactly?" she interjects sharply. "Your secret? The diner? Me?"

I take a step closer, trying to bridge the gap not just in our proximity but in our understanding. "I was protecting a chance to be seen for who I am, not for my family's legacy."

Her laugh is bitter, devoid of any humor. "And what about my chance to see you for who you truly are? You took that from me."

The accusation stings, and I struggle to find the right words. "I know I made a mistake, but my feelings for you, my intentions for the diner—they were never part of any deception."

She shakes her head, the hurt evident in her eyes. "How can I believe that now? Everything is tainted. Your arrival, your interest in the diner, and us. How do I know what's real?"

Her words are a sharp reminder of the rift my secrets have caused. "I'm asking you to give me a chance to make it right. To earn back your trust."

"Trust?" Her voice rises, a mix of anger and pain. "That's not something you can just 'earn back' with apologies and promises. It's built on honesty—something you conveniently forgot."

I reach out, but she steps back, an unspoken boundary between us. "I'm not asking for immediate forgiveness. Just an opportunity to show you the real me, without the shadows of my family's name or hiding my original purpose in coming to Branson."

She looks at me, her expression softening slightly, but the resolve is still there. "I can't. It's too much. I need you to stay away from me and from the diner. I need space to think, to understand how I feel about all of this."

The finality in her words leaves me reeling. "Naomi, I..."

But she cuts me off, a finality in her tone. "Goodbye, Carson."

She turns and points to the outside, indicating I should leave. I do so, and she follows, the door closing quietly behind her before she locks it and walks away without speaking again. I'm left standing in the dimly lit parking lot, the silence around me echoing the void her departure has left.

I stand there for a long time, grappling with the weight of what just happened. The rift between us feels like a chasm now, one I'm not sure can be bridged, but I'm not ready to give up. Not on the diner, not on Branson, and certainly not on Naomi.

As I head into the night, my mind is a whirlwind of thoughts and emotions. Regret, determination, and a deep-seated need to make amends drive me forward. The road ahead is uncertain, but I'm resolved to walk it, to prove my worth, not just to Naomi, but to myself and to the town that's slowly becoming a part of me.

Leaving the diner behind, the night air feels heavy, laden with my thoughts and regrets. I find myself wandering aimlessly until the neon sign of a local bar beckons me. A place to clear my head, or at least to drown the swirl of emotions.

Inside, the bar is a comfortable blend of chatter and clinking glasses. I take a seat at the counter, ordering a whiskey, neat. The liquid burns a trail down my throat, a welcome distraction from the turmoil inside.

Beside me, a man with an easy smile and an air of confidence nurses a beer. He glances over, a spark of recognition in his eyes. "You're the talk of the town, aren't you? The mystery investor. I'm Luke Whitmore." He extends a hand, his demeanor friendly.

I shake his hand, a bit taken aback by the direct approach. "Carson Daniels, and yeah, I guess I am."

Luke chuckles, a twinkle in his eye. "Rumor has it you're trying to blend in. I heard a wild theory that you're related to us Whitmores. Small towns and their stories, huh?"

His comment, meant in jest, hits closer to home than he realizes. I hesitate for a moment, then decide on the truth. "Actually, Luke, the rumors aren't far off. I am a Whitmore—technically."

In the dim light of the bar, Luke's skepticism quickly turns to disbelief. He leans back, eyeing me with a mix of incredulity and irritation. "So, you're a Whitmore, huh? You expect me to believe that? How exactly do you figure?"

The tension between us thickens, the air in the bar charged with an impending storm. "It's complicated." My voice is steady despite rising unease. "Our father... he was involved with my mother before he married yours. I'm your half-brother."

On his other side, a man I hadn't noticed leans over. I recognize him now that he's not hunched over his beer—Jesse, another of my brothers.

Jesse's face reddens, his hands clenching into fists. "That's a damn lie. My dad would never... You're just here to stir up trouble, aren't you?"

I try to explain, to make him understand, but the words are drowned out by his growing fury. "Listen to me, guys, I'm not lying. There's more to this story..."

But they're not listening. Jesse stands abruptly, his chair scraping loudly against the floor, and Luke steps between us, seemingly intent on being the one to lay into me. "You come into our town, spreading lies about my family, trying to weasel your way in? I don't know what your game is, but you better clear out of Branson, and keep your slander to yourself."

The accusation stings, the rejection a blow I hadn't fully anticipated. I stand, trying to reason with him. "Please, just hear me out."

But Jesse and Luke are already storming out, leaving a wake of murmurs and glances in the bar. I'm left standing there, the rejection heavy on my shoulders. This isn't how I wanted things to start off with my brothers.

I realize then the magnitude of what I'm up against—not just convincing Naomi or integrating into the town but facing a family whose history and dynamics are more complex than I'd imagined. Luke and Jesse's reactions, raw and visceral, are a stark reminder of the challenges ahead.

As I step out into the cool night air, the reality of my situation settles in. The path to acceptance, to belonging, is fraught with obstacles and revelations that have the power to divide as much as they reveal.

My resolve to make things right, both with Naomi and with my newfound family, is firmer than ever, but the journey ahead is daunting, filled with rifts that might not easily be mended.

Walking under the starry sky, I dial Ellen, my step-grandmother, the only family member who knows the full story. She answers with her usual warmth, a stark contrast to the cold reception I've just experienced.

"Ellen, it's Carson. I... I tried to talk to Luke Whitmore tonight. I met Jesse, too."

Her tone changes, a note of concern creeping in. "How did it go, dear?"

I recount the encounter, the anger in their voices, their outright denial and accusation. "They didn't believe me. They think I'm here to cause trouble."

Ellen sighs, a sound heavy with empathy. "I feared this might happen. The Whitmores are proud people, Carson. Revelations like this can be challenging."

I lean against a lamppost, the light flickering above me. "What should I do? I came here to connect with my roots, not to tear apart a family."

Her voice carries a reassuring calm over the miles. "This is a journey you have to navigate carefully. Your intentions are good, but the revelation you bring can unsettle long-held beliefs and family dynamics."

I nod, staring into the darkness. "I understand, but it's harder than I thought it would be, and there's Naomi. I don't want to lose her over this."

"You might need to give them all some space. These things take time to process. As for Naomi, be honest with her. Show her your true self and let her make her own decisions."

Her advice feels like a lifeline in the chaos of my thoughts. "Thank you, Ellen. I just wish there was an easier way to handle this."

"Life's important lessons rarely come easy, dear, but remember, you're not alone. You have me, and you have your own strength. Trust in that, and in the truth of your story."

"They wouldn't even let me explain. Our father knew my mother long before he knew theirs. It's like they didn't want to hear anything that might disrupt their view of the world."

Her tone softens. "People often reject what they don't understand, especially when it challenges their beliefs about their loved ones, but you know the truth. In time, with patience, they might come to accept it too."

I sigh. "It's just... I've always felt this gap, Ellen. With Mom and my stepdad gone, there's this sense of... I don't know, loneliness? I thought finding the Whitmores, my blood relatives, would fill that."

"Family connections can be complex. Finding your roots doesn't always provide the immediate sense of belonging we hope for, and sometimes, family isn't just about blood. It's about who we choose to let into our lives."

Her words strike a chord, and I find myself thinking of Naomi. Her laughter, her strength, and the way she makes me feel part of something. "I've found something special in Branson. Not just with the Whitmores, but with Naomi, and with the town. I don't want to lose that."

"Then hold onto it. Work for it. Be patient and stay true to yourself. Your journey is about more than just finding where you came from. It's about where you're going and who you want to be."

I sit down on a nearby park bench, feeling a mix of exhaustion and resolve. "I guess I'm learning that the hard way."

"Often the best lessons are learned that way," says Ellen gently. "Remember, no matter how lonely you feel, you're not alone. You have a story, a history, and now, a future to build in Branson."

We talk a little longer, her wisdom a guiding light in the darkness of my uncertainty. Hanging up, I realize that while I long for a connection with the Whitmores, what I truly seek is a sense of belonging, a place, and people to call my own.

I end the call with Ellen, her words resonating deeply within me. Sitting on the bench, I take a moment to gather my thoughts, to steady the whirlwind of emotions inside. There's a sense of resolve taking shape, a clearer vision of what I need to do next.

I grab my keys and start walking again into the brisk

autumn night, back toward the diner, to reclaim my car. The streets of Branson are quiet, a peacefulness that contrasts sharply with the turmoil in my heart. My car is parked a few blocks away, a solitary figure under the dim streetlights.

As I walk, my mind replays the conversation with Luke and Jesse—if you can call it a conversation—the heated words, the rejection, but Ellen's advice echoes louder, a reminder that this journey is about more than just blood ties. It's about finding where I belong, forging new connections, and building a future.

I reach my car and slide behind the wheel, the familiar space offering a momentary refuge. The engine hums to life, breaking the silence of the night. I take a deep breath, letting the calmness of the moment wash over me.

Driving back to the Chateau on the Lake, where I've been staying, the quiet roads offer a chance to reflect. The lights of the Chateau come into view, its grandeur a welcome sight.

Parking the car, I sit for a moment, looking out at the Chateau. It's beautiful and luxurious, but it feels more like a temporary shelter than a home. Home, I realize, is what I felt beginning to build in Branson with Naomi.

Stepping out of the car, I feel a renewed sense of purpose. The path ahead is uncertain, filled with challenges and potential rifts, but also with possibilities and new beginnings. I'm ready to face whatever comes, to prove myself in Branson, to the Whitmores, and most importantly, to Naomi.

10

STARLIT CONFESSIONS – NAOMI

It's mid-afternoon at the diner, and the lunch rush has just tapered off. I'm wiping down tables when Jenny comes over with a pot of coffee.

"You've been out of sorts these past few days, Naomi," she says, filling my cup. "Is it Carson?"

I sigh, not meeting her eyes. "Is it that obvious?"

She sits down, her expression a mix of concern and frankness. "Honey, it's written all over your face. You miss him, don't you?"

The question hangs in the air, heavy with unspoken truths. "I don't know. After everything that's come out...it's complicated."

"But do you still have feelings for him?" she presses gently.

I nod, a reluctant admission. "Yes, but I don't know if I can trust him again."

She reaches across the table, her hand warm on mine. "Sometimes, we have to take chances, especially with matters of the heart. Maybe he deserves a chance to explain, to make things right."

Her words linger with me for the rest of the day, a gentle nudge toward a decision I'm scared to make. That evening, as I'm closing up, my phone rings. It's Carson, his voice hesitant on the other end.

"Naomi, could we meet at the Chateau? I have something I want to show you, to explain things."

After a moment of hesitation, Jenny's advice echoing in my mind, I agree. "Okay, Carson. I'll be there."

Arriving at the Chateau a while later, I'm ushered through the opulent lobby and up to the rooftop. The door opens to reveal a breathtaking scene—a table set for two, candles flickering softly, and the city lights and the lake sparkling below us.

Carson stands there, looking more vulnerable than I've ever seen him. "I wanted to do something special, to show you how I feel," he says, guiding me to the table.

As I take in the stunning setup, the effort Carson has put into this evening is unmistakable. The rooftop is transformed into a private haven, the cityscape a distant, twinkling backdrop.

Carson pulls out a chair for me, and as I sit, he takes a deep breath. "These past days without you have been a reflection. I've realized how much I need to open up and share my true self with you."

He pours the wine, his hands steady but his voice betraying a hint of nervousness. "I've been afraid that my past and my family's history would overshadow what I'm trying to build with you, but I was wrong to keep it from you."

I listen, my heart a mix of emotions. His honesty is plain, and it starts to thaw the ice around my heart. "I understand your reasons, but it's been hard feeling like there was this part of you I didn't know."

He nods, acknowledging my feelings. "I know I can't change the past, but I want to be open with you from now on. No more secrets, and no more half-truths."

As we eat, the conversation flows more freely. We talk about his fears, his hopes, and what Branson means to him. The more he shares, the more I see the Carson I was drawn to in the beginning.

After dinner, Carson stands and offers his hand. "May I have this dance?"

The soft melody of a song fills the air, and as we dance, the city lights below us seem to fade into insignificance. It's just Carson and me, reconnecting in a dance that feels like a new beginning.

I lift my head instinctively, and his lips brush against mine in a tender kiss that sends a shiver down my spine. It's a promise of what's to come, a reminder of our link, and a symbol of our growing connection. He kisses me again, deeper this time, as if he's savoring the moment. His touch is intoxicating, and I find myself lost in the sensation of his lips on mine.

Carson presses his tongue against the seam of my lips, seeking entry. I part them, allowing him access, and his tongue slips inside, exploring my mouth with a passion that makes my knees weak. I cling to him, my body responding to his touch, and a fire ignites within me, a burning desire that threatens to consume us both.

I'm still slightly wary. Can I trust him? I'm not sure, but my body is fully engaged and seems poised to surrender. His tongue sweeps over mine, and I moan softly, unable to resist the pleasure coursing through me.

My mind is torn, but my body is screaming for more. I want him. I need him.

The kiss deepens, and I feel the last of my resistance crumble. I give in, letting the sensations wash over me.

His hands roam over my body, sending shivers of delight through me. I arch against him, craving more.

He breaks the kiss, his eyes dark with desire. "Are you giving me a second chance to prove myself?"

I nod, my voice husky with need. "Yes, Carson. I am."

He smiles, his expression a mix of relief and passion. "Thank you. I won't let you down."

His words send a shiver of anticipation through me, and I pull him closer, eager to explore this newfound connection. Our lips meet again, and I lose myself in the sensation, the taste of him, the feeling of his body pressed against mine. Part of me thinks this is happening too quickly, and I don't really know him, but desire drowns out that tiny voice of reason.

He pulls back again. "Do you want to come to my room?"

I hesitate, but I want this, want him. I nod, and he leads me down the rooftop stairs to his suite. As soon as we're inside, he pulls me close again, kissing me with a hunger that matches my own. His hands roam over my body, setting every nerve ending alight with need. My heart races, and I can barely breathe as he pushes me against the wall, his lips trailing down my neck.

I gasp, arching against him, and he growls, low and deep. The sound sends a jolt of desire straight to my core, and I'm suddenly desperate for more. I tug at his shirt buttons, my fingers clumsy with impatience. He helps me strip it off, and I run my hands over his bare chest, reveling in the feel of his skin beneath my palms.

He groans, pressing closer, and I can feel his cock, hard and straining against the fabric of his pants. The knowledge that I'm turning him on like this makes me bolder, and I reach down, stroking him through the material. He shudders, his hips bucking at my touch, and I grin, enjoying the power I have over him.

"I want you," he says, his voice husky with need. "I need you."

I nod, my own desire matching his. "Take me."

His eyes flash with lust, and he scoops me up, carrying me to the bedroom. He sets me on my feet, his hands roaming over my body as he kisses me hungrily. I tug at his belt, my fingers clumsy with impatience. He helps me strip it off, and I unfasten his pants, pushing them down along with his boxers. His cock springs free, hard and ready.

I drop to my knees and take him in my hand, stroking his length as I look up at him. He groans, his hips bucking at my touch. "You seem really happy to see me. Is this all for me?"

He nods, his voice husky with need. "Only you."

I lean in, swirling my tongue around the head of his cock. He shudders, his hips thrusting as if seeking more.

"That feels so good."

I smile, taking him deeper into my mouth. He moans, tangling his fingers in my hair as I suck and lick him. The sounds he's making spur me on, and I take him as far as I can, using my hand to stroke what I can't fit in my mouth.

He's breathing heavily now, his body trembling with need. I keep going, wanting to bring him to the edge of release, but before I can, he pulls me up, kissing me hungrily. He pulls down the zipper on my dress, sliding it off my shoulders and letting it fall to the floor. I'm standing there in just my bra and panties, and he takes a moment to admire me.

"You're so beautiful," he whispers, running his hands

over my curves. "I want you so much, and I want to be inside you when I come."

I smile.

"So, I guess this is your last chance to change your mind. Do you trust me enough to stay, or are you going to leave?" There's a hint of challenge in his tone and desperation in his voice.

11

MERGING – CARSON

I hold my breath after saying the words. I need to be sure this is what she wants. I don't want to do anything to screw up this second chance with her.

Her eyes search mine, and I can see the wheels turning in her head. Finally, she nods, her expression serious. "Okay, let's do it."

I feel a surge of relief and excitement as I laugh at her phrasing. "Let's do it? That's how you're going to say yes to spending the night with me?"

She grins, shrugging. "What can I say? I'm a woman of few words."

I chuckle, pulling her close and kissing her softly. "I'll take it, and I promise to make it worth your while."

She wraps her arms around my neck, smiling. "I'm counting on it."

I kiss her again, savoring the taste of her lips as I fumble with the hooks on her bra. Once I've freed them, I pull the lacy garment off, tossing it aside. I step back to admire her, my gaze sweeping over her bare breasts. "You're so beautiful," I murmur, cupping her full breasts in my hands. "I could stare at you all night."

She blushes, biting her lip. "I'd rather you touch me than stare at me."

I grin, leaning down to kiss her again. "Your wish is my command." I trail kisses along her jawline, down her neck, and across her collarbone. She shivers, arching into me, and I smile against her skin. I continue my descent, kissing a path down her chest until I reach her breasts, which I'm still holding in my hands. I circle her nipples with my tongue, teasing them to stiff peaks. She gasps, tangling her fingers in my hair, and I love the effect I'm having on her.

"Carson…" She breathes my name, and my cock twitches in response. I can tell she's getting impatient, so I move lower, kissing my way down her stomach. I pause at her navel, dipping my tongue inside, and she squirms, giggling, as my fingers hook the edges of her lacy black panties.

I slide them down her legs, exposing her glistening center. She's already wet for me, and the sight makes my cock throb with need. I can't wait to be inside her, but first, I want to taste her. I gently push her down onto the bed, spreading her thighs and settling between them. I run my tongue along her folds, savoring the sweet and salty flavor of her arousal. She moans, gripping the sheets as I swirl my tongue around her clit.

I tease her entrance with my tongue before plunging it inside, tasting her fully. She cries out, arching against me as I fuck her with my mouth. Her muscles tighten around me as I drive my tongue deeper into her slick heat. She writhes beneath me, her body trembling with pleasure.

"Oh, Carson…please…" She writhes against me as I move my tongue up her slit, back to her clit. I suck the sensitive bud into my mouth, flicking it with my tongue. Her body tenses, and she lets out a cry as her orgasm crashes over her. I keep licking and sucking, drawing out her pleasure until she comes again. I'd keep going, but my cock is aching with need, and grinding it into the side of the mattress isn't helping stave off the desire to plunge inside her.

I stand up to grab a condom from my bag. She watches me, her eyes heavy-lidded with desire. "Hurry," she says, her voice husky with need.

I tear open the foil packet and roll on the condom before returning to the bed. My cock is rock-hard and ready, and I can't wait to be inside her. She spreads her legs, and I climb on top of her, positioning myself at her entrance. I thrust inside her, and she moans, arching her back as I fill her completely. The sensation is incredible, and I start moving, slowly at first, but soon picking up speed. She matches my rhythm, meeting my thrusts with her own. We move together in perfect harmony, our bodies in sync as we chase our release.

My movements become more urgent as my climax approaches, and her breathing quickens, her nails digging into my back as she nears her own peak. I reach down between us, finding her clit and rubbing it in time with my thrusts. She cries out, her muscles tightening around me as she comes again. The sensation of her inner walls clenching around my cock pushes me over the edge, and I bury myself inside her as I come with a groan.

The world seems to slow as we ride out the waves of pleasure together, our bodies entwined in the aftermath of our lovemaking. I press a kiss to her forehead, and she smiles up at me, her eyes shining with contentment.

"That was wonderful," she whispers, her voice husky with satisfaction.

I grin, brushing a strand of hair off her face. "It certainly was."

We lie there for a few minutes, basking in the afterglow, before I reluctantly get up to dispose of the condom. When I return, I find her curled up on the bed, looking adorably sleepy. I chuckle, climbing back into bed and pulling her close. "Go to sleep, baby. You've had a long day."

She snuggles against me, sighing contentedly. "Mmm, okay. Good night, Carson."

"Good night, Naomi."

I hold her close, listening to the sound of her breathing as she drifts off to sleep. In the quiet that follows, my thoughts settle on her and the possibility of a future before us. I still want to buy her diner, but I know she won't agree to that. Maybe she'll more seriously consider a partnership or a merger instead now? I could again offer to invest in the diner and bring in some fresh ideas to revitalize the business. It would give her a chance to expand her reach while allowing me to be a part of her life.

As I drift off to sleep, visions of the diner and Naomi fill my dreams. I see her smiling at me, her eyes sparkling with love and affection. I see us working together, side by side, creating something special and unique. I've made a billion dollars or more in my career, so the idea of revamping a failing diner shouldn't be so exciting. Of course, it has everything to do with the woman lying beside me.

I WAKE before her despite having fallen asleep after her. The sun is just peeking over the horizon, and I reluctantly wake her. "Do you need to open the diner?"

She grunts and snuggles under the blanket. "Closed on Mondays."

I chuckle, wrapping my arms around her and pressing a kiss to her temple. "I'm glad you said that, or I would've felt guilty for stealing your time."

She turns in my arms, her eyes blinking open with clear reluctance. "I'm trying to sleep."

I laugh at how grouchy she sounds. "How does someone who's clearly not a morning person manage to own and run a diner?"

She shrugs and yawns. "Coffee. Lots of coffee."

I chuckle, kissing her forehead. "I'll make sure you have plenty of coffee today, if you'll spend the day with me."

She sighs, snuggling closer to me. "Okay, but I need to get up and shower. I'm gross and sweaty."

I grin, running my hand down her back. "I don't know, I kind of like you like this."

She swats at me playfully, rolling out of bed. "I'm going to take a shower."

I watch her walk to the bathroom, admiring the view. "Want some company?"

She glances back at me, a mischievous glint in her eyes. "Maybe."

I follow her into the bathroom, unable to resist the temptation. I step into the shower behind her, wrapping my arms around her waist and pulling her close. She leans back against me, sighing contentedly as the warm water cascades over us. By the time we finish, the water is lukewarm. Considering the size of this resort, and the first-class accommodations, it must take a long time to deplete the supply enough to notice.

When we're dressed, and I'm ordering breakfast from room service, I'm surprised to realize we spent more than an hour in the shower, making love and learning more about each other's bodies. I'm already looking forward to spending the rest of the day with her, exploring more of Branson if we bother to leave the room.

First, I want to discuss my idea of a partnership between us—business first, though the idea of being her partner in all things is seductive in a way I've never experienced before. No woman has tempted me to settle down. Until now.

"What's the plan for today?" she asks as she sips her coffee. "I thought I'd show you around town. There's a great little market where you can pick up some fresh produce and baked goods."

I smile at the thoughtfulness of her suggestion. "That sounds perfect, and afterward, maybe we could head back here and spend the afternoon in bed?"

She raises an eyebrow at me. "Are you planning on wearing me out, Carson Daniels?"

I lean over and kiss her softly. "Absolutely. I intend to make the most of every minute we have together."

She smiles against my lips. "In that case, I'd better eat a big breakfast so I have plenty of energy."

I take her hand. "Before we do anything else, I want to talk to you. I have a proposition."

Her eyes widen, and I chuckle. "Not that kind of proposition. Although, if you're interested, I'm always game."

She smacks my arm playfully. "Stop teasing me. What's this proposition of yours?"

I take a deep breath, gathering my courage. "I've mentioned it before, but I figured I'd offer again, since things are different now. I want to invest in the diner. Not buy it, but invest in it. Bring in some fresh ideas, update the menu, fix the sign out front, and put in some new lighting inside. The place has a ton of potential, and with the right marketing and branding, we could really turn it into something special."

She frowns, shaking her head. "I appreciate the offer, but I'm not interested in selling the diner. It's been in my family for generations, and I'm not about to give it up just because some fancy businessman from the city thinks he can swoop in and save the day."

I roll my eyes. "It's not a savior complex. I want to help you because I like you, and the diner has a lot of potential. I'm talking more about being a silent partner with some suggestions and input. I'm not suggesting I buy it, as I just said. I know you won't go for that and understand now that I know the history and its importance to your family and this community."

She sighs, running a hand through her hair. "I don't know if that's such a good idea. I mean, what happens if things don't work out between us? It could get messy, and I don't want that for the diner. It's already struggling enough as it is."

I reach out and take her hand. "I understand your concern, and I promise that I would never do anything to jeopardize the diner. If things between us don't work out, then we'll figure out a way to make it work. We'll have a contract, and our business partnership will be strictly separate from anything else."

She bites her lip, considering my offer. "I guess it couldn't hurt to hear you out, but I'm not promising anything. I'm just saying that I'll listen to what you have to say."

I grin, leaning in and kissing her cheek. "That's all I'm asking for right now." I spend the next half-hour giving her some ideas and researching numbers as we talk. By the time

I've given her my on-the-fly presentation, she seems as excited about the idea as me.

"So, you're saying I'm still the boss? Whatever I decide is final say?"

I nod, grinning. "Of course. This is your diner, and I'm just offering my expertise and resources to help you make it the best it can be."

She smiles, reaching out and taking my hand. "I think we can make a pretty good team."

I squeeze her hand, returning her smile. "I know we can."

We spend the rest of the day brainstorming ideas for the diner. By the time we're finished, we have a solid plan for the renovations, along with a new menu and branding. I can't wait to get started on the project, and Naomi is just as eager. We never make it out of my suite, and I order dinner for us from room service. "This reminds me of the first time Ted let me take lead on a solo project."

She frowns. "Who's Ted?"

"My stepfather. I called him Dad when we weren't at work." A grim smile touches my lips for a moment. "He was a dad in all the ways that count, and losing him was rough. I guess it's part of why I came to Branson, to see if my biological father could measure up to Ted, only to learn he passed away already too."

She pats my hand, her expression gentle. "There's still a possibility of getting to know your brothers."

I sigh and tell her about my brothers' reactions. "You can see why I'm not too optimistic."

She frowns. "I'm sorry. I wish I could say something to make it better, but I know from experience that time and patience can heal a lot of wounds. Just keep trying to get to know them if it's important to you."

I nod, appreciating her advice. "I will, though I'm not sure how receptive they'll be."

She squeezes my hand, her eyes full of compassion. "Wyatt is a big softie under his tough exterior, and I'll speak to Fallon. She can get her husband to do anything, including sitting down and talking to you. Luke tends to be a bit more hotheaded in general, so it's no surprise he didn't give you a chance to say much. I think Jesse will come around once Luke does."

I smile at the thought of Naomi intervening on my behalf. "Thank you. I'd appreciate that."

She kisses me softly. "Let's get some sleep. We have a busy day ahead of us tomorrow."

I pull her closer, enjoying the feel of her body against mine. "I guess I should set an alarm?"

She groans but nods. "Five a.m."

I whistle through my teeth. "Good thing I'm a morning person."

She glares at me, but her lips are twitching. "I'm not."

I kiss her forehead. "I'll make sure you have plenty of coffee. That usually helps, right?"

She smiles, nodding. "Yes, that usually helps, but I'll bet you can think of an even better way to wake me up…"

I grin. "I'm sure of it."

12

SHATTERED PEACE – NAOMI

I jolt awake to the sharp crunch of shattering glass. It's been a few nights since I first spent the night with Carson, and word has slowly spread through town about us being together. Heart pounding, I throw off the covers and race to the front window of my apartment, which sits right across from the diner. In the dim glow of the street-lamps outside, I see a lone dark figure dart away as more crashes split the night air.

"Carson, wake up. Someone's vandalizing the diner," I shout.

He jolts up from the bed, instantly alert. We exchange one dismayed glance before rushing outside in our pajamas into the cold night. Rounding the corner of the diner, my breath catches at the damage. Jagged glass blankets the side-walk amidst ruined pies and our splintered saloon-style door. The front windows gape open with angry red paint streaking down the remaining panes, condemning my collaboration with Carson.

My heart races, a tight knot of fear and anger forming in my chest as I survey the wreckage. Carson is beside me, his expression a mirror of my shock. The once welcoming facade of the diner is now a scene of devastation, with the hateful message scrawled in angry red paint.

"Get out, Daniels!"

I feel Carson's hand on my shoulder, a silent gesture of support. "I'll call the police," he says, his voice steady despite the chaos. He's already dialing the sheriff while I start picking up the larger pieces of glass, the sound sharp and jarring in the quiet morning air.

Sheriff Bigsby arrives swiftly, his expression grim as he takes in the scene. "Naomi, Carson, I'm sorry to see this. We'll start an investigation right away."

I nod, brushing a strand of hair from my face. "Sheriff, I have a suspicion it might be Mr. Jenkins. He's been openly hostile toward Carson, and with us spending time together recently, it makes sense he'd target the diner."

The sheriff nods thoughtfully. "We'll look into it, but let's not make any hasty accusations. I'll need to talk to him and see if anyone else saw anything."

Carson steps forward, his voice firm. "I want to help however I can, Sheriff. I don't want Naomi or her business to suffer because of me."

Sheriff Bigsby pats him on the shoulder. "I know, son. We'll get to the bottom of this. In the meantime, I suggest keeping a low profile, for both your sakes."

After the sheriff leaves, Carson and I are left in the silent aftermath. The damage seems more real now, more personal. It's not just about broken glass. It's about someone trying to shatter the peace of this place I love.

Carson helps me board up the windows, his movements methodical and focused. "I can't tell you how sorry I am. If this is because of me..."

I cut him off, placing a hand on his arm. "We don't know

that for sure, but what I do know is that we won't let this break us. We're stronger than some coward's hateful message."

He looks at me, admiration, and something deeper in his eyes. "You're so strong, and it's one thing I admire about you."

Together, we clean up the remaining debris, the diner gradually taking shape again, albeit scarred. The sun rises higher, casting a warm glow over the damaged but not defeated space.

As we finish, I realize the gravity of what's happened. It's not just a random act of vandalism. It's a targeted message against Carson and what we're building together.

The morning progresses with a surreal quality, the damaged diner a stark contrast to the normalcy of Branson waking up. Regulars approach, their expressions a mix of concern and disbelief.

Mrs. Henderson, the pie contest champion, comes first, her hands clasped over her mouth. "Oh, Naomi, this is just terrible. Who would do such a thing?"

I force a smile, despite the ache in my chest. "I don't know, Mrs. Henderson, but we'll get through this. The diner's seen worse."

She nods, her eyes watery. "You're a strong one, dear. If there's anything I can do, just say the word."

As she leaves, Mr. Simmons, the local postman, stops by. "Heard about the ruckus. Anything I can do to help, Naomi?"

"Thanks, Mr. Simmons," I say, grateful for the support. "We're managing, but I appreciate the offer."

The morning is filled with similar exchanges, each one a small reminder of the community's solidarity. It's heartening, yet the undercurrent of what caused this lingers heavily.

By midday, we've cleared a lot of the debris, and I've arranged for a glazier to replace the windows. The diner looks bare and vulnerable without its familiar glass panes, but it's a necessary step toward rebuilding.

We're still cleaning up when Fallon stops by, her brow furrowed in concern. "Naomi, this is awful. How are you holding up?"

I lean against the wall of the diner, watching Carson continue to sweep, as the fatigue of the day sweeps over me. "I'm okay, Fallon. Just... overwhelmed, but Carson's been a big help."

Fallon's gaze is suddenly wary. "Yeah, about Carson..."

I groan softly. "Have you spoken to Luke? I guess he's told you—"

"That Carson claims to be his, Wyatt, Jesse, and Raylan's brother. Yeah, he told us." Her lips are set in a grim line. "Luke outright rejects the idea, and so does Raylan. And Frankie says Jesse doesn't even want to discuss it. They're heading out on a trip for the veterans' project tomorrow, so I think the other three will have to sort all this out and Jesse will have to trust them."

"And your husband?"

She hesitates. "I don't think Wyatt knows what to think or even wants to think about it."

I sigh, running a hand through my hair. "I was afraid of that. Carson told me his claim to be the Whitmores' half-brother didn't go over too well."

Fallon shakes her head, arms crossed. "That's an understatement. Luke refuses to even entertain the idea, and Raylan sees Carson as an interloper upsetting the family dynamic."

I chew my bottom lip, considering. Fallon has always had a moderating effect on her rugged husband. Maybe she can persuade Wyatt to at least hear out Carson. Even just meeting without punches or accusations thrown could diffuse some of the tension seething under the town's surface lately. I decide to gently press the notion.

"I hate to ask this, but do you think you could convince Wyatt to maybe sit down with Carson sometime? No drama, just talk. It might help resolve some bad blood if the eldest Whitmore brother would hear him out." I hold my breath, praying I haven't overstepped some boundary by including her in her husband's family disputes.

Fallon glances away, conflict playing subtly across her face. After a weighty pause, she exhales and looks back at me. "You know Wyatt can be overprotective toward his siblings, but he's not closed minded. I think he'd be willing to size him up man to man at least. I'll suggest it to Wyatt and see if he'll bend."

Relief floods through me. If stubborn yet noble Wyatt agrees to a civil discussion, Carson's odds of integrating himself eventually into his estranged father's family might improve drastically, and if my diner's recent troubles prove anything, some unity against outside threats could serve us all.

I reach out to squeeze Fallon's hand gratefully. "You clearing the path for conversation again would mean the world, Fallon Wyatt listens to you most."

She smiles gently. "He'd better, since I'm his wife, and I don't know that he listens much when he's got some bone-headed notion sometimes, but I'll remind him keeping tensions from boiling over can only help the family, and you." Her eyes take in the diner's damage pointedly. "We protect our own around here."

I swallow thickly, once more moved by the caring bonds tying our community together. With Fallon newly allied to my cause, I'm buoyed by hope that soon Carson might find a place with his brothers, or at least work toward common ground.

The sun beams brightly by the time Carson and I clear the last shards of glass from the sidewalk. Despite the light warming my face, I still feel chilled, my arms wrapped tight around my torso. Carson stands and places a gentle hand on my shoulder.

"Why don't we get cleaned up while we wait for the glazier?"

I nod, suddenly feeling just how grubby I am after hours of sweeping and scrubbing paint flecks from brick and wood. As we head upstairs to my little apartment, I catch my reflection in a shard still clinging to an outer window frame. Haunted eyes stare back from a paint-smudged face. The violation sweeps over me anew, and I hasten inside, desperate to scrub away external signs of inner turmoil too.

Under the steady stream of hot water however, tears slowly mix with clinging suds as the trauma of last night sinks in fully at last. I muffle sobs, irrationally fearful of appearing weak, but soon the shower curtain edges back. Carson's strong arms wrap around me without a word, liquid proof of my anguish washing away down the drain along with his own soap.

After a long moment, I finally find my voice. "I just keep wondering if that message was meant for you, or for any newcomers wanting to update elements around here. Either way, it feels like a personal attack on our hopes too."

Carson smooths back my wet hair to meet my eyes. "I wish I could promise no one will react badly again as changes come that we can't even foresee yet, but together, we're strong enough to weather any storms. I know it." He brushes his lips tenderly over my forehead. "And if anyone tries threatening your dream again, they'll regret it." Quiet steel underpins his tone.

Comforted, I lean into him, the steady beat of his heart and drum of water lending familiar rhythms to settle my still-frayed nerves. As the worst of the sting washes away down the drain, I know Carson speaks truth—together we are strong enough to withstand ignorant resistance and keep fighting for the place and people we care for.

We finish showering and dry off. I put on warm sweats, still feeling a bone-deep chill that's purely emotional at this point. Carson has no fresh clothes, so he puts on what he wore earlier. "You should stay with me instead of at the Chateau—or at least bring over some clothes."

His gaze lights up, but before he can respond, the echo of a truck rumbling over loose gravel outside pulls my gaze to the doorway. A beat-up Ford pickup with "Joe's Glass" on the door is pulling into the diner's parking lot.

Carson glances my way. "That'll be Joe with our new windows. Want me to walk out with you to discuss installation?"

I nod gratefully, spirits bolstered by having someone beside me during this whole ordeal. We head out to find Joe already unpacking replacement panes from protective wrapping.

"Good afternoon, Naomi. I'm sorry to see some fool went vandalizing a community treasure this way," says Joe by way of greeting. His grizzled features are etched in sympathy beneath the faded cap shading his eyes.

"We appreciate you coming so quick to patch her up," says Carson with a polite hand extended. "I'm Carson, Naomi's business partner and, regrettably, the reason she was targeted."

Joe gives Carson's hand a brisk shake, peering a little

closer at him. "You the newcomer I been hearin' about stirring up old timers around the pub? Can't say I hold stock with their grumbling over change. Known Naomi here long as she's been alive and know she got a good head on those shoulders."

I can't help but flush a little at Joe's grandfatherly praise, but it heartens me to have his solid faith marking today's damage as an aberration in our friendly community, not the new norm. As Joe starts carefully replacing the first windowpane, I breathe deeper, peace settling in my soul once more.

This diner stands as evidence of persevering through harder times before, and just like Joe sealing out damaging elements with steadfast care and new glass, Carson and I will face unsettled detractors together while still welcoming the whole town inside these repaired walls soon enough.

As the last pane slides perfectly into place, sunlight streams unbroken over the counter once more. I slip my hand into Carson's, our twined shadows stretching over the familiar tiled floor. This new glass feels symbolic—a fresh start for us and for all of Branson toward healing rifts.

With vandals and fear mongers alike unable to dim my hopes now, I squeeze Carson's hand, joy and resolution swirling together inside. The future awaits, brighter than ever.

13

COMMUNITY EMBRACE – CARSON

I'm surprised when Naomi asks me to accompany her to the local church for a town hall meeting. After the recent vandalism, I assumed some residents would still be wary of my presence, but she assures me that the pastor and many loyal patrons want to show support.

We're barely through the doors when Clara, a regular customer, engulfs Naomi in a fierce hug. "Oh, honey, I came as soon as I heard. Don't you worry, we'll have the place fixed up good as new."

Naomi returns her embrace, smiling. "You're too kind, Clara. We've pretty much restored it to running shape, but just having everyone rally together means the world already."

As we take our seats, more well-wishers stop by, clasping Naomi's hand or patting my shoulder in encouragement. Their genuine care for each other and for this cherished community hub moves me. The pastor invites Naomi up to say a few words, and her voice rings with resilient strength and pride in her family's legacy.

When Sheriff Bigsby provides an update, I brace myself

for scrutiny, but he simply requests information on anything unusual locals might see. Murmurs of support continue rippling through the crowd.

The most rousing moment comes when grey-haired Joe, the glazier, stands to propose a fundraising drive to cover damages. "Naomi's folks have run that fine establishment for generations now. It's high time we showed support 'fore some vandal scares her off! I say we pitch in to get that diner shipshape again."

A standing ovation follows as Naomi dabs at glistening eyes. We stay late helping organize volunteer efforts and tidy up the cheerful chaos. As we finally head to our cars, she turns to squeeze my hands, smile radiant even in the darkness.

"This is the true heart of Branson, Carson," she says simply. My own chest swells in turn, moved by this community's authenticity.

THE NEXT AFTERNOON as I'm buying wood finish from "Harry's Hardware," I sense someone behind me and turn to see Wyatt watching me, stroking his bearded chin thoughtfully. Before I can speak, he gestures outside, where we sit together on a truck bed, springs creaking slightly.

I explain about the letters my mother left me, detailing her romance with Carson Senior, who she described as a charming businessman who made her feel truly special before returning home to Missouri.

Wyatt shifts on the truck bed, brow furrowed. "So, you're telling me my father had a prior relationship down in Texas that produced a son he never knew about?"

I meet his piercing gaze. "I know it sounds improbable,

but my mother left me letters confessing the truth before her passing. Carson Whitmore spent over a month in Dallas on business ventures when she worked as a corporate coordinator. They had a passionate affair that meant the world to her."

I explain how she raised me alone to allow Carson Senior's budding relationship here in Branson to bloom without interference. My stepfather was a loving dad, but after his death, I finally went digging into biological family ties, uncovering evidence leading me here.

Wyatt listens intently, sharp eyes evaluating my timeline against his own recollections. "And you say you found letters from this woman laying out the circumstances around your conception definitively implicating my father?"

I nod. "I was shocked reading them myself, but it all adds up. I know this disrupts assumptions about your family narrative, but I'm not here to cause turmoil. Only to connect with my roots if possible."

Wyatt strokes his beard, gazing toward the lake pensively. I brace for more skepticism over upending his perceptions of their family history, but his next words surprise me.

"Life has a way of humbling even the most stubborn notions over what 'truth' means sometimes, doesn't it?" He meets my hopeful eyes. "It'd be foolish not to offer some hospitality and see what comes of it." He extends his hand, callouses rough but grip warm. "Supper tomorrow then?"

I exhale in relief and gratitude, shaking firmly. "I look forward to it."

He claps my shoulder and gestures down the street. "I'm meeting up with Raylan for lunch at Naomi's diner. Why don't you join us, and we can all talk?"

I nod, and we make our way toward the familiar diner

facade just down the block. Being midday, the place is bustling when we step inside. Naomi looks up from behind the counter where she's pouring coffee for one of her regular customers. She gives me a subtle smile before returning her focus to the patron.

Wyatt leads us toward a corner booth. As we slide into the worn red leather seats, I catch a glimpse of Naomi laughing with an elderly couple at the counter. Her smile lifts my spirits even as perky Jenny comes by to take our orders.

Wyatt and I have just received our cheeseburgers when the entrance bells jangle loudly. I glance up to see Raylan striding in. Raylan pulls up short at the sight of me sitting with Wyatt, his expression stormy. He grabs a chair from another table and swings it around, straddling it backward to face us. His steely gaze remains unimpressed as he looks at me.

"Word going around town is you've been making some claims about being our pa's long-lost son," he says, direct and to the point. His tone drips skepticism. "When I caught wind of that, I figured I should hear the story straight from the source."

His tone remains skeptical, but I keep my own measured as I respond. "I realize it seems unlikely for someone to show up out of nowhere claiming a relationship after all these years, but I have documentation supporting my mother's connection to Carson Whitmore while he was traveling."

Raylan lifts a thick brow. "Our father happened to father some mystery kid that no one ever knew about until now, huh?" He uncrosses then re-crosses his muscular arms across his broad chest. "I built my fortunes understanding human motivations well. So lay out these so-called facts and let me interpret their likelihood."

I meet Raylan's challenging gaze. "I wouldn't fault your skepticism, but these letters my mother left tell a convincing tale, if you'll allow me to relay it."

At his subtle nod, I unfold the yellowed pages with Amelia's flowing script detailing when she first met the elder Carson Whitmore over thirty-seven years ago.

"Mother had just started working as an office coordinator at a prominent law firm in Dallas when your father flew in to oversee a lucrative merger deal..." I summarize the whirlwind weeks she spent giving Carson senior tours after hours, their passionate trysts in his penthouse suite.

"In her words, their romance made her feel truly seen and cherished for the first time." My fingers trace the faded ink proclaiming declarations of being soulmates cruelly torn apart by obligations back home in Missouri.

I meet Raylan's piercing eyes. "When she realized she was pregnant after he'd already departed, Mother agonized over contact but ultimately kept her condition secret to avoid further fallout."

Raylan shifts. "Even if this far-fetched affair occurred, perhaps your mother misremembered my father as the culprit in all that melodrama." His tone still rings skeptical but no longer carries such outright hostility at least.

I retrieve a photograph capturing Amelia and Carson Senior locked in an intimate embrace with a familiar balcony vista behind them. Even Raylan cannot deny our father's features matching the smitten man nestled against my beaming mother bathed in the glowing Dallas sunset.

Raylan takes the photograph, studying it. The skepticism in his eyes softens, replaced by a hint of recognition. "Well, I'll be... Dad did have a life outside of Branson, it seems." He hands the photo back with a newfound openness. "Guess it's time we find out the truth, scientifically."

I nod, relieved by his response. "A paternity test would give us definitive answers."

"Let's get it done then," says Raylan, standing up with a newfound pragmatism. "I'll arrange a visit to the clinic tomorrow. We'll know soon enough if you're really a Whitmore."

Wyatt, who's been quietly listening, rises and places a hand on my shoulder. "In the meantime, Carson is going to join us for dinner tomorrow night, so you'll be there, Raylan?" At his brother's nod, he says to me, "Bring Naomi along too. Her opinion matters in all this."

I feel a surge of hope at his words. "Thank you, Wyatt. I'd appreciate that, and Naomi will have some interesting insights for sure."

As Naomi walks over, her anxious expression eases as Wyatt updates her on the plan. She smiles, her hand landing warmly on my shoulder. "I'm glad we're taking steps to sort this out. I have a good feeling about it."

Her support feels good, and I cover her hand with mine, grateful.

Wyatt smiles, nodding in approval. "We'll see you both tomorrow. Looking forward to some family revelations and maybe welcoming a new member to the fold."

As they leave, I feel a mix of anticipation and relief. The path forward is clear, and with Naomi by my side, I'm ready to face whatever the results might reveal. I'd be far more shocked if the DNA tests show we aren't siblings, so I'm already thinking ahead to the future, to building connections after they accept we're related.

14

A PLACE IN THE FAMILY – NAOMI

The Whitmore family dinner is a tableau of apprehension and curiosity as we gather around the long dining table. The rich aroma of roasted meat and seasoned vegetables fills the air, but it's the undercurrent of unspoken questions that dominates the room.

Carson, sitting beside me, takes a deep breath before addressing the family. "Thank you for having us tonight. I know my presence raises a lot of questions. I want to share something with you all," he says, his voice steady but tinged with emotion.

He pulls out a stack of aged letters, the handwriting elegant and flowing. "These are letters from my mother, Amelia, written to me as a keepsake, and I guess as a way to tell me the truth of the matter after she was gone, since she never mentioned it while she was alive. They detail her relationship with your father, Carson Whitmore Senior, and how I came to be."

The room is silent, all eyes on Carson as he reads excerpts from the letters. Carson's hands tremble slightly as he unfolds the first letter, the paper thin and delicate. He clears his throat and begins to read, his voice carrying the weight of decades past.

"'Carson,'" he reads, "'My first meeting with your father was like a scene from a movie. He walked into the law firm with such confidence, yet when our gazes met, there was an instant connection, an unspoken understanding that we were meant to cross paths...'"

I watch the family as they listen, their expressions shifting from skepticism to intrigue. Amelia's words, spoken through Carson, paint a vivid picture of two people caught in a whirlwind romance.

"'We would meet after hours,'" Carson continues, "'Wandering through the streets of Dallas, talking about everything and nothing. Those nights were magical, a secret world just for us. I remember laughing in his arms under the Texas stars, feeling like the happiest woman alive...'"

The atmosphere in the room softens, the initial tension giving way to a quiet empathy. Luke, who had been the most doubtful, now leans forward, his earlier hostility replaced by curiosity.

"'But then he had to leave,'" Carson reads on, "'And though my heart broke, I understood. Your dad had a duty to his family in Branson and responsibilities that were a world away from our stolen moments in Dallas. He was the caretaker for his widowed mother, and his career was in Branson. Mine was in Dallas...'"

Wyatt, usually stoic, shows a flicker of emotion. "Sounds like Dad had a whole other life before he settled down with Mom," he says, more to himself than anyone else.

Carson places down the letters, meeting their eyes. "When my mother realized she was pregnant with me, she was torn. She came to Branson to tell Carson Senior when she was about six months along only to learn he'd recently gotten back together with his ex-girlfriend and was engaged to her—your mother." His voice cracks for a moment.

He looks down at the letters again. "She wrote here about her struggle and her decision to keep it a secret, to protect both me and your father from scandal and safeguard his future with his fiancée. She left without seeing him because she didn't want to break up their relationship or cause him problems with the woman he planned to marry when my mother wasn't prepared to move to Branson, and Carson Senior couldn't move to Dallas. In the end, she decided it was best that no one know."

The room is quiet, each person digesting the story and the reality of Carson's connection to their family. It's Luke who breaks the silence. "I... I never would've guessed. Dad always seemed so...grounded in Branson, and he was crazy about Mom."

Carson nods, understanding. "My mother loved him, and in her way, she was trying to honor that by staying away."

The revelation in Carson's words seems to linger in the air, wrapping around the room like a gentle embrace. There's a shift in the dynamic, a sense of barriers beginning to crumble.

Wyatt speaks up, his voice thoughtful. "It sounds like she was a remarkable woman, Carson, and it seems you've inherited some of that strength." Wyatt leans back in his chair, his gaze contemplative. "You know, if what you say is true, then you're part of this family's story. A chapter we never knew existed."

Carson looks around the table, his eyes meeting mine. "All I've ever wanted was to find where I belong. To connect with my roots. Tonight, sharing this with you, it feels like I'm taking the first step toward that."

Raylan seems to be reassessing his initial skepticism. "Well, if Dad had this whole other life, who are we to deny it? I mean, it's a lot to take in, but...maybe it's time we open our minds a bit."

Luke, however, remains stoic, his arms crossed. "It's a nice story, but I need more than old letters to convince me. Dad was a man of principle. He wouldn't just..."

Wyatt interrupts him gently. "Luke, sometimes people have chapters in their lives we know nothing about. It doesn't change who they were to us. It just adds more depth to their story."

"He wouldn't cheat on Mom."

"He didn't," says Carson softly as he sorts through the letters and hands one to Luke. "She lays out the timeline clearer here. As you can see, Carson Senior had broken up with his girlfriend a few months before meeting my mom. He got back together with her when he returned to Branson."

Luke reads it, and he seems a little less tense after a moment. "If they weren't together for a spell, it's not cheating."

"Would you mind telling me more about Carson Senior?" asks Carson, taking my hand as though fearing their rejection. I squeeze reassuringly.

The brothers have no problem talking about their dad and mom, and as the evening progresses, the dining room of the Whitmore household resonates with the warmth of shared stories and newfound connections. Carson, with a mix of nervousness and excitement, delves deeper into his past when Raylan asks.

"I grew up in a small town in Texas, in a suburb outside of Dallas, where my mom was an attorney. It was just me and her for a long time. She gave me a world full of love and did her best to make up for being my only parent until she met Ted, my stepfather. She always made time for me no matter how busy she was prepping for a trial."

Wyatt, his expression softening, nods in understanding. "Dad was the same way. He might have been busy with the business, but he always made time for us."

Raylan, leaning back in his chair, adds with a chuckle, "Yeah, like the time he took us camping and we ended up getting lost in the woods. Remember that, Wyatt?"

Wyatt laughs, a genuine, hearty sound. "How could I forget? We wandered for hours before finding our way back. Dad pretended he knew where he was going the whole time."

The room erupts in laughter, the shared humor a balm to the earlier tension. Carson smiles, feeling more at ease. "My mom and I used to go stargazing. She'd tell me stories about the constellations, making up tales about heroes and adventures."

"That sounds wonderful," says Wyatt, his tone reflective. "Dad loved the stars too. He used to say they were like guides, leading us through life."

The conversation shifts to family holidays, each sharing their fondest memories. Raylan recounts a hilarious mishap during a Fourth of July barbecue, where a firework display went comically awry.

Carson joins in, sharing a story about his first Christmas with Ted as his new stepfather, and how he was still unsure about him until Ted gave him a sneaky driving lesson on his ATV.

As plates are cleared and dessert is served, the mood in the room is light, almost celebratory. The initial apprehension has given way to a sense of camaraderie and understanding.

Luke, who has been quietly listening, finally speaks up again. "Hearing all this...I think we might have more in common than I first thought."

Carson turns to him, clearly surprised but pleased. "I hope so, Luke. I've always wanted to connect with my father's side of the family."

The evening winds down with an air of acceptance and newfound familial bonds. Carson's journey, once filled with uncertainty, now finds a sense of closure and belonging within the Whitmore family. They seem to have accepted him even without the DNA results, but I already know they have to be brothers. They have too many similarities not to be related.

As we stand to leave, Wyatt extends a warm hand to Carson. "You're part of this family, Carson. Let's make up for lost time."

Carson shakes his hand, a smile of gratitude spreading across his face. "I'd like that very much. Thank you."

The drive back to my apartment is filled with a comfortable silence, the events of the evening settling around us like a gentle fog. Carson seems more at ease, a lightness in his demeanor that wasn't there before.

As he pulls up outside my place, I turn to him, my heart full of emotions from the night. "Do you want to come in?" I ask, hoping he feels the same connection that's been growing stronger between us.

He looks at me, his eyes reflecting the soft glow of the streetlights. "There's nowhere else I'd rather be right now."

Inside, the familiarity of my apartment feels even more welcoming with Carson by my side. We sit on the couch, close yet not touching, the air between us charged with unspoken words.

"I never thought I'd find a place in the Whitmore family," says Carson softly, breaking the silence. "Tonight felt like a turning point."

I reach for his hand, intertwining our fingers. "You'll soon feel like you belong, I think. Sometimes, family is more about the connections we forge than the ones we're born into."

He turns to me, his hand squeezing mine. "And what about us, Naomi? Where do we stand in all this?"

I lean closer, the proximity sending a thrill through me. "We're writing our own story. One that's just beginning."

He smiles, a genuine, heartfelt smile that lights up his face. "I like the sound of that."

Our conversation drifts to dreams, hopes, and the future we might build together. It's a future filled with possibilities, with challenges and joys waiting to be discovered.

As the night deepens, he leans in, his lips meeting mine in a kiss that's tender and full of promise. It's a kiss that speaks of new beginnings, of shared paths, and of a bond that's grown stronger through adversity and understanding.

We spend the night wrapped in each other's arms, the outside world fading away. In these quiet moments, I realize how much Carson means to me, how he's become an integral part of my life.

Morning finds us still entwined, the first rays of sunlight creeping through the curtains. As I stir, Carson's eyes open, a sleepy smile spreading across his face.

"Good morning," he whispers, his voice rough with sleep.

"Good morning," I reply, my heart swelling with happiness. "Ready to face a new day together?"

He nods, pulling me closer. "With you by my side, I'm ready for anything."

15

LOVE SURPRISE – CARSON

The diner, usually alive with the sounds of clinking dishes and laughter, is quiet tonight. It's after hours, and I've arranged a special evening. My heart races with a mix of nervousness and excitement. I'm not going to propose. It's not that time yet, but tonight, I plan to tell Naomi something deeply true and personal—I love her.

The tables are neatly rearranged to create an intimate space in the center of the diner. Soft, ambient music fills the air, a selection of romantic tunes setting the perfect mood. Candles are lit on every table, their flames flickering gently, casting a warm and inviting glow.

I'm fidgeting with a small velvet box in my pocket. It's not a ring—it's too soon for that—but a vintage locket, elegant and timeless, just like Naomi. I want to give her something that symbolizes the depth of my feelings.

The bell over the door chimes, and Naomi steps in. She pauses, taking in the scene. "Carson, what is all this?"

I take a deep breath and walk toward her. "This place is

where our story began, and I wanted to share something important with you here."

I lead her to the center of the room. The flickering candlelight plays across her face, accentuating her beauty. I take the velvet box from my pocket and hold it out to her. "Before I say anything, I want you to have this."

Her hands cover her mouth as she opens the box, revealing the locket. "Carson, it's beautiful, but why?"

I take her hands in mine, steadying my voice. "Because I've realized something since we've been together. I love you. I've fallen completely and utterly in love with you."

For a moment, she's speechless, her eyes shining with unshed tears. Then, a radiant smile breaks across her face. "I love you too. I didn't know if it was too soon to say it, but I feel the same."

Relief washes over me, mixed with a joy I've never felt before. I pull her into my arms, and we sway gently to the music, surrounded by the soft glow of candlelight. As the soft music crescendos before going to another instrumental piece, I lower my head and kiss her deeply, pouring all my love and emotions into the kiss. She responds eagerly, her body molding to mine as we lose ourselves in the moment.

We continue dancing, our bodies moving in sync as I breathe in her familiar scent. It's a heady mix of vanilla and spice, and I find myself wanting to drown in it. Her hair tickles my chin as I bury my face in it, inhaling deeply. She smells like home, like everything I've ever wanted and more. My lips instinctively find hers again, and we sway to the music as I kiss her with all the hunger coursing through me. There's no holding back. Not anymore.

As the last notes of the current song fade away, I reluctantly break the kiss, resting my forehead against hers. "I could stay like this forever," I whisper, my voice thick with emotion.

She smiles. "Me too, but we're going to end up making love, so we should go across the street to my apartment. I can't imagine boinking in the diner."

A startled laugh escapes me. "Boinking? What a charming turn of phrase."

She grins. "It's accurate though, isn't it?"

I nod, grinning back at her. "Very accurate."

We gather our belongings, blow out the candles, and lock up the diner, walking hand in hand across the quiet street to her apartment. As we step inside, I pull her close, kissing her deeply. She responds eagerly, her body molding to mine as we lose ourselves in the moment.

I lift her effortlessly, carrying her to the sofa. We tumble onto it, laughing and kissing as we struggle to remove each other's clothes. Her skin is soft and warm beneath my touch, and I can't get enough of her. I kiss my way down her neck, savoring the taste of her. She moans softly, arching against me as I cup her breasts, teasing her nipples with my thumbs.

"That feels so good." She sighs, her eyes half-closed in pleasure as I ease off her shirt, and the pink bra beneath it. I pause to admire the sight of her, her skin flushed with desire and her lips slightly parted with anticipation.

"You're so beautiful." I whisper, leaning in to kiss her again. She runs her hands over my bare chest, sending shivers of delight through me. I reach for the waistband of her jeans, unbuttoning them slowly and sliding them down her hips. As I peel off the last of her clothing, I take a moment to appreciate the perfection of her naked form. She's perfect, and she's mine.

I trail kisses along her inner thighs, drawing closer to

her center. She lets out a gasp of pleasure as I press my tongue against her slick folds, tasting her sweet nectar. She arches against me, her fingers tangling in my hair as I explore her most sensitive areas.

"More." She pants, her voice heavy with desire. Her body is trembling with need, and I'm more than happy to oblige.

I slide a finger inside her, feeling her muscles clench around me. She's so wet and ready, and I can't wait to be inside her again. I add another finger, curling them to hit that spot that drives her wild. She cries out, her body shuddering as I swirl my tongue around her clit.

I keep up the rhythm, driving her higher and higher until she's on the verge of release. Then, I withdraw, leaving her panting and desperate for more.

"Why did you stop?" Naomi's voice is husky with desire.

I lean down, my lips brushing against her ear. "Because I want to be inside you when you come."

She gasps, her eyes darkening with desire. "Then what are you waiting for? You're wearing way too many clothes."

I grin, stripping off my shirt and pants in record time. She gazes at me appreciatively, her eyes roving over my naked body. I can't wait to feel her skin against mine as I take a condom from my wallet and roll it on. I climb on top of her, my cock throbbing with need.

I position myself at her entrance, teasing her with my tip. She writhes beneath me, her hips bucking impatiently. "Please, Carson..."

I can't hold back any longer. I thrust into her, groaning as her tight sheath envelopes my cock. It feels so right to be inside her, joined together as one. We both moan in pleasure, our bodies moving in sync as we find our rhythm.

She wraps her legs around me, urging me deeper. I pick

up the pace, my movements becoming more urgent. I cant my hips, driving into her, and she cries out, her nails digging into my back. I'm lost in the sensations—the feel of her body beneath mine, the sound of her moans, and the scent of our lovemaking. It's all too much, and I'm on the verge of losing control.

I grit my teeth, trying to hold back, but she's so damn sexy and responsive. She's begging for more, her voice hoarse with desire. I can't resist her, and I give in to my own need, thrusting harder and faster while reaching between us to stroke her clit. It doesn't take long before she's coming apart, her muscles clenching around me as she cries out in ecstasy.

The sensation of her climax triggers my own, and my vision blurs as I spill myself inside the condom, almost resenting the latex barrier between us. I want to be fully connected to her, skin to skin. It's a powerful, almost primal release, and I collapse on top of her, spent and satisfied.

We lie there for a few moments, our breathing ragged and hearts pounding. Finally, I muster the energy to roll off her, disposing of the condom and pulling her close. She rests her head on my chest, and her breath tickles my skin as she snuggles against me on the couch.

"That was intense," she says with a contented sigh.

"It was perfect." I stroke her hair, reveling in the feel of her in my arms.

"Mmm, it was." She traces lazy circles on my chest with her fingertip. "I'm glad we were able to work things out."

"Me too." I press a kiss to the top of her head, breathing in the scent of her shampoo. "I don't know what I would've done if I'd lost you after just finding you."

She tilts up her chin to look at me. "I love you, Carson Daniels, and I'm so glad you found your way to Branson."

"I'm glad I did too." I brush my lips against hers, savoring the taste of her. "I couldn't imagine my life without you in it. I love you and always will."

Too replete to move to the bedroom, we fall asleep in each other's arms right there, content in the knowledge that we're exactly where we belong.

16

RENOVATION DREAMS – NAOMI

The early morning light filters through the windows of the diner, casting a fresh, new glow on the familiar space. Today is special—Carson and I are starting the renovations we've been dreaming of and planning for the past two weeks, which means the diner is closed for a while. It's more than just a refurbishing of the diner. It's a symbol of our growing life together.

We stand amidst the old booths and worn-out decor, plans in hand. "So, what do you think about going for a retro vibe for the booths?" I ask, pointing to the designs we've been mulling over.

Carson leans over, his dark hair falling slightly into his eyes. "Retro sounds great, but let's add a modern twist. Maybe some sleek lines to go with the classic look?"

I nod, excited by his input. "Perfect blend of old and new. Just like us, huh?"

He grins, a playful spark in his eyes. "Exactly, and what about the color scheme? Are we thinking bold or more subdued?"

"Bold," I say instantly, "Like reds and blues. It'll give the place a vibrant, lively feel."

As we discuss, we move through the diner, envisioning the changes. Our laughter echoes in the empty space, evidence of the ease and joy we find in each other's company.

Carson picks up an old, faded chair, examining it. "We could repurpose these, give them a fresh coat of paint, and maybe some new upholstery?"

I nod. "That's a great idea. It keeps a piece of the diner's history alive."

The morning progresses with us deep in discussion, selecting materials, and finalizing designs. Our ideas flow seamlessly together, a dance of creativity and collaboration.

We take a break, sitting on the counter with coffee in hand. Carson looks around, a contented smile on his face. "This is going to be amazing. I can't wait to see it all come together."

I lean against him, feeling a surge of happiness. "Me neither, and doing this with you makes it even more special." I fiddle with the vintage locket he gave me, its weight a comforting reminder of his love. "I've been thinking," I say, breaking the comfortable silence between us, "What if we started hosting community events here? Like local art shows or poetry readings?"

Carson, who's been sipping his coffee, looks up with interest. "That's a brilliant idea, and live music nights. Imagine this place filled with music and life."

I smile at his enthusiasm, feeling the creative energy between us. "It'd be a great way to bring the community together and make the diner a real hub like it used to be in my great-grandfather's day."

Our break ends, and we move through the diner, planning as we go. Our ideas bounce off each other, growing and evolving. I point to a corner. "What about making that a small stage area?"

He nods, walking over to examine the space. "Perfect. It could be a cozy spot for musicians or poets."

As we start clearing out the old furniture, there's a comfortable, easy rhythm to our work. We lift, carry, and stack, moving in sync. It's hard work, but doing it together makes it enjoyable.

Our laughter and chatter fill the diner as we work, the sound of our combined efforts a melody of its own. Every so often, Carson reaches out to brush a strand of hair from my face or to steal a quick kiss, each touch sending a flutter through my heart.

By the end of the day, we're tired but satisfied. The old furniture is cleared out, and the space ready for its transformation. We stand together, looking around at the empty diner, imagining what it will become.

In the now empty space, Carson suggests, "How about we cook up something? All this work's made me hungry."

I nod, already heading toward the kitchen. "I'm on it. How do you feel about hashbrowns and sandwiches?"

"Perfect," he says, following me.

In the kitchen, the warmth and familiar scents bring a cozy feeling. I start grating potatoes while Carson gathers ingredients for the sandwiches. We move around each other effortlessly, the kitchen space feeling intimate.

Carson playfully nudges me as he reaches for the bread. "I think I've become quite the expert sandwich maker since meeting you. I used to leave most of that to my housekeeper, but now, I can throw toppings together with bread like a pro."

I chuckle, elbowing him back gently. "Oh, really? I'll be the judge of that."

The sizzle of the hashbrowns fills the air as I focus on not burning them. Carson, meanwhile, is assembling the sandwiches with an exaggerated concentration that makes me laugh.

"Watch and learn, Naomi," he says, winking at me.

I shake my head, smiling. "Such a show-off."

As the food cooks, the playful banter continues. Every now and then, our hands brush, sending little sparks of electricity between us. He steps closer at one point to 'inspect' my hashbrowns. His proximity sends a warm rush through me. He leans in and plants a soft, teasing kiss on my neck.

I lean into the kiss for a moment, then playfully push him away. "Hey, I need to focus here. We can't have burnt hashbrowns on your watch, Mr. Expert."

He laughs, raising his hands in surrender. "All right, all right. I'll behave... for now."

We finish cooking, and the simple meal looks perfect. We sit at a makeshift table in the middle of the empty diner, surrounded by our plans and dreams.

The food is delicious, but it's the company that makes it special. We talk and eat, the conversation flowing as easily as the laughter. After we're done, Carson helps me clean up. As I wash the dishes, he stands behind me, wrapping his arms around my waist.

"This," he whispers in my ear, "Is everything I ever wanted. You, us, this place...our future together."

I lean back against him, feeling content and full of love. "Me too, Carson."

We finish cleaning up and lock the diner. The evening air is crisp as we step out of the diner, and Carson pulls me closer, his hand warm in mine. The street is quiet, the world around us feels peaceful, almost as if it's holding its breath in anticipation of our future.

"Every moment with you feels like a step toward something wonderful," Carson says, his voice soft in the quiet of the night.

I look up at him, the streetlights casting a soft glow on his face. "I feel the same. It's like we're building our own little world, and I love it."

As we walk, a comfortable silence settles between us, filled with the unspoken bond we share. Our steps are in sync, mirroring the harmony we've found in each other's company.

We reach my apartment, and Carson stops, turning to face me. He brushes a lock of hair behind my ear, his touch gentle and familiar. "These past weeks with you have been some of the happiest of my life. I can't wait to see what the future holds for us."

I reach up, pulling his face down to mine, our lips meeting in a kiss that's full of love and promise. When we part, I whisper, "Let's make every moment count."

He smiles, his eyes shining with emotion. "With you, every moment already does."

We enter my apartment, leaving the quiet street behind. Inside, the world is ours, full of dreams, plans, and a love that grows stronger with each passing day..

Inside my apartment, the familiar coziness envelops us. Carson and I move through the space with an easy grace, a reflection of our growing intimacy and understanding. I flick on the lights, casting a warm glow over the room, and head to the kitchen to make us a late-night cup of tea.

Carson follows, leaning against the counter as he watches me. "You know, I used to think moments like these were just ordinary, but with you, they're anything but. They're the moments I treasure the most."

I smile, handing him a steaming mug. "It's the little things, isn't it? The quiet nights, the shared laughs, and the cups of tea. They all add up to something pretty special."

We settle onto the sofa, our bodies instinctively finding a comfortable position nestled together. The tea warms us, but it's the closeness that truly brings comfort.

Carson raises his mug in a small toast. "To all our future ordinary moments that we'll make extraordinary together."

I clink my mug against his, feeling a surge of affection. "To us."

We talk for hours about everything from the diner's renovation to our hopes and aspirations. Our conversation is a tapestry of shared dreams and plans, woven with laughter and tender glances.

Eventually, the clock ticks toward the early hours of the morning, and our conversation slows, the comfortable silence settling around us like a blanket.

Carson yawns, his eyes still fixed on me. "I should probably head back to the hotel," he says reluctantly.

I reach for his hand, not ready for the night to end. "Stay."

He looks at me, a question in his eyes, then slowly nods. "I'd like that. I'd like that very much."

We stand, holding hands, and move toward the bedroom. The world outside fades away, leaving only the two of us, wrapped in the magic of our love.

As we lie down together, the night wraps around us, a cocoon of peace and intimacy. In Carson's arms, I feel safe, cherished, and deeply loved. In the quiet of the night, as we drift toward sleep, I know that every step we take together is a step into a future bright with love and possibility.

17

DOUBTS AND DECISIONS – CARSON

The sound of renovation fills the diner, a tangible sign of change. Amidst the hum of activity, I find myself grappling with a growing unease, sparked by a snippet of conversation I accidentally overhear between Naomi and Jenny.

I'm in the storage room, organizing old diner memorabilia when their voices drift through the half-open door.

"...it's a big step, Naomi." Jenny's voice is laced with concern. "Bringing Carson into the business, I mean. Are you sure it's the right move?"

There's a pause before Naomi replies, her voice slightly hesitant. "I believe in Carson, Jenny. He's been great, but yes, it's a risk, and I'd be lying if I said I wasn't a little nervous about it."

The words hit me like a physical blow. Doubt, like a creeping shadow, begins to cloud my thoughts. Does Naomi really have faith in me? Or am I just a convenient addition to her plans?

For the rest of the day, I try to shake off the feeling, but it clings to me, coloring my interactions. Naomi notices something is off, but I dismiss her queries with a strained smile. "Everything's fine," I say, avoiding her probing gaze. "Just a lot on my mind, you know?"

But it's not just the renovations that are weighing on me. It's the fear of being an outsider in Naomi's world, a fear that her faith in me might not be as strong as I believed. The tension between us grows, an unspoken undercurrent that neither of us addresses. We work side by side, but there's a distance that wasn't there before.

A couple of nights later, as we're closing up, the strain becomes too much to bear. Leaning against the diner's door, I feel a knot of anxiety in my stomach.

Naomi approaches, her brow furrowed with concern. "Carson, talk to me. What's going on? You've been so distant."

I hesitate, torn between revealing my fears and keeping them hidden. "It's nothing. Just renovation stress, I guess."

But the truth is, it's more than that. It's a gnawing doubt about my place in her life, about whether I'm truly a part of her world. We walk to her apartment in silence, each lost in our own thoughts. I know I should open up to her and clear the air, but the fear of her response, of confirming my doubts, holds me back.

That night, in bed, the distance between us feels more profound than ever. She reaches out to me in the darkness, but I turn away, lost in a whirlwind of uncertainty.

The next morning, I wake up early, my mind a roiling sea of doubts. I watch Naomi sleeping peacefully, her calmness in stark contrast to the turmoil in my heart. Quietly, I slip out of bed, needing space to think. After dressing, I head out for a walk. The streets are deserted, the pre-dawn quiet echoing my internal chaos.

As I walk, I wrestle with my decision. Do I confront

these doubts head-on and talk to Naomi about what I over-heard? Or do I continue to let this uncertainty fester between us, unspoken but ever-present and slowly poisoning what's good between us—if there's really something good between us. If she has doubts about me, can she really love me as she claims?

The early morning light slowly brightens the streets, painting the world in hues of gold and pink, but the clarity I seek remains elusive, my mind a maze of fear and indecision. By the time I return to the apartment, Naomi is awake, concern etched on her face. "Where were you? I woke up and you were gone."

I stand there, torn. This is my chance to open up, to bridge the gap that's formed between us, but the words stick in my throat, fear and doubt holding them back. "It was just a walk to clear my head," I say finally, the half-truth feeling heavy on my tongue.

Naomi studies me, her gaze searching. "There's something you're not telling me, Carson. Whatever it is, we can talk about it. We're in this together, remember?"

Her words, meant to be reassuring, only serve to deepen my inner conflict. Yes, we're in this together, but can I truly be a part of her world, her dreams if she's having doubts? "I know," I say, forcing a smile. "I'm just... trying to figure some things out."

Naomi steps closer, her hand reaching for mine. "Figure it out with me. Whatever it is, we can handle it."

I look at her, at the trust and love in her eyes, and feel a pang of guilt for my unvoiced doubts, but the fear of what her answers might be, of what my questions might reveal, keeps me silent.

As I nod in agreement, the words I need to say remain unspoken, the doubts and decisions still swirling in my heart, an unresolved melody in the symphony.

THE NEXT DAY at the diner, the air is thick with the electric buzz of saws and the rhythmic thuds of hammers, yet an invisible tension still hovers between Naomi and me. She's bustling around, coordinating with the contractors, her usual vibrancy slightly dimmed. I'm helping out where I can, but my movements are mechanical, my mind a tumult of unresolved emotions.

Mid-morning, she approaches me with a concerned look. "Carson, are you sure you're okay? You seem... off."

I force a smile, trying to dispel the worry in her eyes. "I'm fine. Just a little tired. You know, long days and all."

She doesn't seem convinced but nods, turning her attention back to the work at hand. I watch her for a moment, admiring her dedication and drive. She's amazing, and that's what makes this uncertainty so painful.

As the day progresses, our interactions are polite, but the easy banter that usually flows between us is conspicuously absent. I catch Jenny watching us with a furrowed brow, clearly sensing the shift in dynamics.

Lunchtime rolls around, and I find myself in the kitchen, prepping sandwiches for the crew. Naomi joins me, her presence a balm and a torment all at once.

She reaches for a tomato, her hand brushing mine, and for a brief moment, our gazes meet. There's a question in hers, a silent plea for me to open up. I break the contact, focusing on the task at hand.

"Let's make sure everyone gets fed," I say, trying to sound upbeat. "They're doing great work."

She nods, her attention on slicing the tomato. "Yeah, they are. This place is going to look incredible."

The rest of the meal prep passes in silence. We work side by side, but the connection we usually share feels strained, like a string pulled taut, ready to snap.

As we serve the food, the crew's gratitude and light-hearted jokes provide a brief respite from the tension, but it's a temporary relief. The underlying current of unease between Naomi and me remains.

In the afternoon, I find myself alone for a moment, leaning against the counter, lost in thought. The weight of my unspoken fears feels like a physical burden, dragging me down.

Naomi comes back in, wiping her hands on a cloth. She pauses, looking at me with a mix of affection and concern. "Whatever it is, you can talk to me. We've always been honest with each other, except for when you didn't tell me about your other purpose for being here."

I look at her, torn between my desire to share my fears and the dread of what it might lead to. "I know, and I appreciate that. It's just... stuff I need to work through on my own."

Her expression falls slightly, hurt flickering in her eyes. "Okay. If that's what you need."

The rest of the day is a blur of activity. The sound of renovation fills the diner, but the music of our laughter and shared joy is noticeably absent.

As we lock up in the evening, the gap between us feels wider than ever. Naomi hesitates at the door, as if wanting to say something more, but then she just sighs, offering me a small, sad smile.

"Goodnight, Carson." She doesn't invite me to her apartment tonight.

I can't blame her after the day of distance between us. "Good night, Naomi," I say, my heart heavy.

As I drive back to the Chateau, the streets empty and quiet, I feel a deep sense of isolation. My doubts and fears have created a chasm between us, and I'm unsure how to bridge it.

In bed that night, I lay awake, staring at the ceiling. The silence is deafening, a stark contrast to the laughter and conversations that usually fill my nights with Naomi.

The realization hits me hard—my inability to share my fears might cost me the most important person in my life, but the fear of losing her, of being inadequate, keeps me trapped in a cycle of doubt and indecision.

As the night stretches on, I know I have to make a choice. Do I let my fears win, or do I find the courage to face them, to talk to Naomi, and to trust in the strength of our love? The answer seems clear, but taking that step feels like the hardest thing I've ever had to do.

Lying in the quiet darkness, my mind churns with the possibilities of what could happen if I reveal everything to Naomi. The fear of rejection, of confirming my worst doubts, is paralyzing. Yet, the thought of losing her because of my silence is even more unbearable.

The memories of our time together flood my mind—the laughter in the diner, the tender moments shared, and the way her eyes light up when she smiles all feel so precious and vital. I can't let my insecurities ruin what we have, and what we could have.

In the early hours of the morning, a resolve begins to form within me. I need to face my fears and talk to Naomi. Our relationship, built on honesty and openness, deserves that much. Keeping these doubts to myself is only creating a barrier between us, one that could grow insurmountable if left unchecked. Today, I *will* talk to Naomi. I'll share my fears and insecurities. It's a risk, but one I need to take. Our future, our happiness, hinges on the strength of our trust and communication.

With the new day comes a new determination. I won't let my doubts dictate our relationship. I choose to fight for us, for the love we share, and for the future we're building together. The first step is honesty, and I'm ready to take it.

18

MISUNDERSTOOD MOTIVES – NAOMI

I've started to notice a change in Carson over the past few days, a shift in his demeanor that I can't quite put my finger on. He seems distant, his usual enthusiasm dampened by an underlying current of distraction.

It first becomes apparent during our routine morning meeting at the diner, where we discuss the day's renovation plans. "Carson, what do you think about the color scheme for the front area?" I ask, trying to gauge his opinion.

He glances at the swatches I'm holding, his response lacking its usual fervor. "They're fine. Whatever you think is best."

I frown slightly, puzzled by his lack of engagement. This isn't like Carson. He's always been so involved and passionate about this project.

As the day progresses, his distant behavior continues. He's physically present, assisting with the renovation, but there's a disconnect in his actions. It's as if his mind is elsewhere.

I try to break through his aloofness during lunch. "Carson, is everything okay? You seem...off."

He offers a strained smile, brushing off my concern. "Just a lot on my mind, Naomi. Nothing to worry about."

But I am worried. This isn't like him. His withdrawal is creating a subtle strain between us, an unspoken tension that's starting to affect our collaboration.

In the afternoon, I attempt to involve him in a decision about the diner's new lighting fixtures. "These vintage-style lights could really add to the ambiance. What do you think?"

He looks at the catalog I'm holding but seems to barely register it. "Sure, they look great."

Frustration bubbles up inside me. His indifference is unlike anything I've experienced with him before. It's as if he's pulling away, and I don't understand why.

Later, as we're working on refinishing some of the old furniture, I accidentally knock over a can of paint. It splashes onto the floor, a bright splotch against the old tiles.

"Dammit," I mutter, reaching for a rag. Carson is quick to help, but even this simple interaction feels fraught with tension. "Sorry," I say, my frustration evident. "Just a bit clumsy today."

"It's okay," he replies, his tone neutral, but I can tell there's something more, something he's not saying.

The rest of the day passes in a similar pattern. We work side by side, but there's a disconnect, a barrier that wasn't there before. Conversations are brief, functional, and lacking the warmth and ease we usually share.

As we lock up for the evening, I can't help but feel a sense of unease. The diner, usually a place of joy and shared dreams, now feels like a stage for our unspoken frustrations. The next couple of days are virtually a repeat, and by that night, I'm tired of asking what's wrong or trying to get him to open. Instead of inviting him to my apartment, I just tell him good night and stand awkwardly.

Carson says good night as well, his farewell brief and perfunctory. I watch him walk away, a knot of concern growing in my stomach.

That night, alone in my apartment, I replay our interactions, trying to decipher what's changed. It's as if a cloud has descended over us, casting a shadow on our relationship.

Over the next couple of days, Carson's withdrawal continues, his once vibrant presence reduced to a shadow of its former self. I find myself treading carefully around him, unsure of how to bridge the gap that's formed. Our collaboration, once a source of strength and excitement, now feels strained, the joy of our joint venture overshadowed by unspoken doubts and misunderstandings. I stop asking him to come to my apartment, feeling like our relationship is in the early death throes.

THE NEXT MORNING, I arrive at the diner with a renewed sense of purpose. The resolve from the previous night has solidified into a determination to address the widening gap between Carson and me. The diner is quiet as I unlock the door, the morning sun casting long shadows across the floor.

He arrives shortly after, his usual greeting subdued. The air between us is heavy with unspoken words. Today, I decide, those words need to find their voice.

As we start our work, I make another attempt at conversation, seeking to rekindle the spark that once came so easily to us. "I was thinking about the menu redesign. Maybe we could try some new recipes and add a bit of spice to the old favorites?"

He nods, his response lacking his typical eagerness. "Sounds good. You always have the best ideas."

It's a compliment, but it falls flat, lacking the genuine warmth I've come to cherish. I sigh inwardly, missing the connection we once shared so effortlessly.

Throughout the morning, the pattern continues. Our interactions are functional, but the joy that once underpinned our teamwork is conspicuously absent. I can't shake the feeling that Carson is holding back something, a barrier that I can't seem to break through.

As the day unfolds, every attempt I make to engage him feels like it's met with a polite but firm wall. Whether it's discussing the new lighting setup or rearranging the seating, Carson's participation is minimal, his mind seemingly elsewhere.

By late afternoon, the diner's transformation is well underway, but the transformation in our relationship feels like it's moving in the opposite direction. The frustration within me grows, a mix of concern and the sting of rejection.

As we're finishing up for the day, I decide to take one more shot at breaking through the barrier. "Carson, can we talk? Really talk? I feel like there's a distance between us that wasn't there before. We need to fix it before we can't."

19

TENSION IN THE AIR – CARSON

The day at the diner is charged with an almost palpable tension. Every word, every glance between Naomi and me feels laden with unspoken emotions. The air is thick with the weight of our growing disconnect, and it's becoming increasingly difficult to navigate.

As the day progresses, the strain only intensifies. I find myself second-guessing every interaction and every decision. The once joyful process of renovating the diner now feels like an uphill battle, with Naomi and me on opposing sides.

The silence between us is broken only by the necessary communication to get through the day's tasks. It's functional, yet devoid of the warmth and connection that once defined our relationship. I miss the laughter, the easy banter, the sense of being in perfect sync with her. I'd planned to talk to her today, but my courage seems to desert me each time I open my mouth.

By the time we close up for the evening, the strain has reached its breaking point. Naomi turns to me, her expression a mix of frustration and concern. ""Carson, can we talk? Really talk? I feel like there's a distance between us that wasn't there before. We need to fix it before we can't. What's going on?"

I hesitate, torn between my desire to open up and the fear of what that might lead to. "Naomi, I... I overheard your conversation with Jenny the other day. About the risks of our partnership, and about your doubts."

Her eyes widen in realization, and then soften. "You misunderstood. Yes, there are risks, but that doesn't mean I don't believe in us, and in what we're doing here. I have faith in you, in *us*."

The words hit me with the force of a bomb. All this time, I had let my doubts and fears cloud my judgment, misinterpreting her concerns as a lack of faith in me. Iv'e been an idiot, stewing in my doubts and fears when a brief conversation would have cleared up everything. Am I trying to sabotage a chance at happiness? I can't believe I am, but I'm doing a good impression of that kind of foolishness.

The tension that's been building between us breaks, giving way to a rush of emotions. I step closer to her, the need to bridge the gap between us overwhelming me. "I'm sorry. I let my insecurities get the best of me. I should have talked to you about it."

She reaches out, her hand gently touching my arm. "We all have doubts. What matters is that we face them together."

In that moment, something shifts between us, the walls of misunderstanding crumbling down. I pull her into my arms, our bodies fitting together as if drawn by a magnetic force.

Our frustration and tension give way to a passionate embrace, a physical expression of our reconciliation and reaffirmed feelings. Our kiss is deep and full of the emotions we've been holding back, a mingling of relief, love, and renewed connection.

When we finally part, there's a new understanding between us. "I love you, Naomi," I whisper, my voice thick with emotion.

"And I love you, Carson," she replies, her voice steady and sure. "No more doubts, okay? We're in this together."

As we lock up the diner and step out into the cool evening air, there's a sense of peace between us, along with a renewed sense of purpose. The challenges of renovating the diner and of navigating our partnership suddenly seem manageable again, as long as we face them together.

"Do you want to stay at my place tonight?" she asks, still seeming hesitant, as though bracing for me to reject her overture.

"Definitely. I don't want to spend another miserable, lonely night without you." I draw her close, the need to feel her body against mine overwhelming as we walk across the street to her apartment. Once inside, our passion ignites, the tension of the days spent arguing and distant giving way to a powerful, fiery reconnection.

She pushes me against the wall, her mouth crashing onto mine as our tongues tangle in a frantic dance. My hands roam over her curves, pulling her closer, as if trying to merge with her very essence. She moans into the kiss, the sound sending a jolt of desire through me.

I lift her up, her legs wrapping around my waist as I press her back against the wall. I grind my hips against her, the rubbing of our bodies creating a delicious friction.

"God, I've missed you." I trail kisses down her neck.

"I've missed you too. So much." Her voice is breathless,

her fingers tugging at my hair as I nip at her collarbone. "Let's never fight again."

"Deal." I capture her lips in a searing kiss, pouring all my love and longing into it. She responds with equal fervor, her body arching against me as I run my hands down her back, pulling her closer. We move in a frenzy of need and desire, our bodies coming together in a symphony of passion. It's as if we're trying to make up for lost time, to reclaim the connection that's been missing between us.

Somehow, I manage to find enough composure to navigate from the wall to her bedroom, setting her down on her feet on the floor beside it so we can undress. She tugs at my shirt, and I hastily unbutton it, letting it fall to the floor. She runs her hands over my bare chest, her touch sending a shiver of pleasure through me. I kick off my shoes and pants, desperate to feel her skin against mine. She pulls me down on top of her on the bed, wrapping her legs around me as I bury myself in her heat.

"Yes. Just like that." Her nails dig into my back as I thrust into her, our bodies moving in perfect sync. The world falls away, leaving only the two of us, joined together in this moment of pure bliss. I lose myself in the sensation, letting go of everything else. It's just her and me, our hearts beating as one, our souls entwined.

I'm not sure how long we stay like that, caught up in each other, but eventually, the urgency of our movements slows, replaced by a tenderness that speaks to the depth of our feelings for each other. We hold each other close, savoring every second, knowing that this is only the beginning of the rest of our lives together.

I remember to pull out at the penultimate moment, since we were in too big a rush for a condom. She smiles and kisses me softly, her eyes shining with love and contentment. I feel the same way, my heart full to bursting with happiness.

"I love you, Carson."

"I love you too, Naomi." I kiss her forehead and hold her close, relishing this precious moment of closeness. I hate that we spent the last few days at odds over a simple misunderstanding and my own internalized fears and insecurities. I won't let that happen again.

THE FOLLOWING day dawns with a renewed sense of hope and connection between us. The misunderstandings and tension that had clouded our relationship seem to have dissipated, replaced by a stronger bond forged through our honest confrontation.

As we arrive at the diner, the atmosphere is noticeably lighter. The morning sun streams through the windows, casting a warm, inviting glow over the renovation-in-progress. "Ready for another day of making this place amazing?" she asks, her voice filled with the enthusiasm I've missed.

"Absolutely," I say, returning her smile. "I feel like we can accomplish anything together."

We start the day with a planning session, sitting amidst the half-painted walls and new fixtures. Our conversation flows easily, filled with ideas and mutual understanding. I suggest a new layout for the dining area, and Naomi builds on it, her creative flair complementing my practical approach perfectly.

As the morning progresses, we work side by side, our renewed connection evident in every shared task and laugh.

The joy of working together, which had been overshadowed by our recent tensions, returns in full force.

We break for lunch, and I decide to surprise Naomi with her favorite—homemade sandwiches and a fresh salad. As we eat, we chat about everything from diner menus to our plans for the evening. The ease of our conversation reminds me of how right it feels to be with her, to share both the mundane and the extraordinary.

In the afternoon, we tackle the task of selecting artwork for the diner walls. Naomi's artistic eye leads the way, but she seeks out my opinions, valuing my input. We find ourselves in agreement more often than not, our tastes and visions aligning seamlessly.

As we stand back to admire our choices, she leans into me, her hand finding mine. "I'm so glad we talked things out. I hate thinking we almost let a misunderstanding come between us."

I squeeze her hand, grateful for her understanding and forgiveness. "Me too. I promise to be more open in the future. No more hiding behind my doubts."

The rest of the day flies by, filled with productivity and laughter. We finalize some key design elements and even manage to finish painting the walls. The diner is transforming before our eyes, a reflection of our own evolving relationship.

As evening approaches, and we start to clean up, Naomi looks at me with a twinkle in her eye. "How about we continue this at my place? I could use some help making dinner."

I laugh, already looking forward to spending the evening with her. "I'm at your service, Chef Naomi."

We lock up the diner and walk to her apartment, our hands entwined. The challenges of the day seem trivial compared to the joy of being together, of knowing that we're on the same page again.

That night, as we cook dinner together in her cozy kitchen, the simple act of making a meal feels like a celebration of our love and partnership. We talk, we laugh, and we plan for the future—a future that seems brighter and more promising with each passing moment.

As we sit down to eat, the candlelight flickering softly between us, I realize how much Naomi means to me. She's not just my partner in business but in life. Together, we've weathered misunderstandings and emerged stronger, more connected, and even more in love.

20

REBUILDING BRIDGES – NAOMI

In the aftermath of our recent reconciliation, I realize that mending our relationship requires more than just resolving a misunderstanding. It needs a foundation built on openness and trust. With that in mind, I plan a surprise evening at the diner, intending to lay bare my hopes and fears about our partnership and future together.

The evening arrives with a soft autumn breeze, and I set up the diner after hours. I arrange a small, intimate table in the middle of the newly renovated space, surrounded by the soft glow of candlelight. It's simple yet speaks volumes about the evening I have planned. I'm trying to mirror the night he told me he loved me for the first time, and I think I'm pretty close to replicating that.

Carson walks in, returning from a made-up errand I sent him on with a box of nails in hand, surprise etched on his face as he takes in the scene. "What's all this?"

I take his hand, leading him to the table. "I wanted to create a special space for us, a place where we can talk openly about everything—our partnership, our future, and everything."

He smiles, the warmth in his eyes reflecting the candle-light. "This is perfect. Thank you."

We sit down, and I take a deep breath, gathering my thoughts. "The last few days made me realize how important it is to communicate, to really understand each other's hopes and fears."

He nods, his attention fully on me. "I agree. We can't let misunderstandings get in the way of what we're building here."

Encouraged by his response, I continue, "I want to be completely honest with you. The diner is a huge part of my life, and bringing you into it was a big step for me, but it's a step I don't regret. My only fear was losing what makes this place special, but I realize now that you're only adding to it."

Carson reaches across the table, his hand covering mine. "I never want to change what makes this diner—or you—so special. I'm here to build something with you, not to take over."

I feel a surge of relief, his words easing the lingering doubts in my heart. "And I want that too. I see how much you care, how much you put into this place. It means the world to me."

The conversation shifts to our personal aspirations within this joint venture. "I want to ensure that while we grow, we keep the essence of what makes this diner unique," I say earnestly. "It's not just about business. It's about creating a place that feels like home for everyone who walks in."

Carson takes a thoughtful sip of his coffee. "I completely agree. It's about preserving the soul of the diner while giving it our own touch. We're not just business partners but care-takers of this special place."

As we delve deeper into our discussion, a comfortable

ease settles between us. The tension of the past few days feels like a distant memory, replaced by a mutual understanding and a shared goal.

At one point, he leans forward, his expression serious. "I want you to know that I'm committed to this, to us. Whatever the future holds, I'm here for the long haul."

I smile, touched by his sincerity. "I feel the same. We're building something beautiful here, together, and I can't imagine doing it with anyone else."

Our conversation gradually winds down as we talk about more immediate plans for the diner. The candlelight flickers, casting a warm glow over us, symbolizing the reignited spark in our relationship.

As we stand to leave after blowing out the candle, Carson hesitates, a thoughtful expression on his face. "Thank you for tonight. It means a lot to have this open communication between us."

I reach out, squeezing his hand. "It's important to me too. We're stronger when we're honest and open with each other."

We leave the diner a few minutes later, the quiet streets of Branson stretching out before us. I feel a sense of contentment and excitement for what lies ahead. Our future is here, growing this diner and our lives together in this town I love.

We walk to my apartment and enter together, both collapsing with tired sighs. As we settle deeper into the couch, wrapped in the comfort of each other, the conversation with Carson takes a more emotional turn. He begins to share more about his past, about the void that Ted and Ellen helped fill, but also about the lingering sense of something missing in his life.

"I was around ten when Ted came into my life," he says, his voice carrying a reflective tone. "He wasn't just a stepdad. He was the father figure I desperately needed. He and Ellen gave me a sense of family, a sense of belonging, but..."

He pauses, looking away for a moment as if gathering his thoughts. "Even with their love and support, there was always this gap, this piece of my identity that felt...incomplete."

I reach out, gently squeezing his hand. "It sounds like they were wonderful people, Carson."

He nods, a faint smile appearing. "They were, Naomi. They really were. Ellen's still the bedrock in my life, but finding out about my biological father, about the Whitmores is like a puzzle piece I didn't even know was missing until now."

The vulnerability in his voice tugs at my heart. "And your brothers? How do you feel about them?"

Carson sighs, turning to face me. "I'm cautiously optimistic. They seem open to getting to know me, which is more than I could've hoped for, but we're still waiting for the DNA results. It's this weird limbo, you know?"

I nod, understanding the complexity of his emotions. "It's a big step, finding and connecting with a family you never knew you had, but I have no doubt DNA will reveal you are brothers."

"I don't really either." He looks down, then back up at me. "Having you by my side through this has made all the difference. You've been my anchor in all this uncertainty."

The sincerity in his eyes makes my heart swell. "I'm here for you however and whenever you need me."

His gaze softens, and he continues, delving deeper into his thoughts about family. "Family has always been a bit of an abstract concept for me. With Ted and Ellen, I felt love, but there was always this part of my history, my identity, that was missing. Now, with the Whitmores, it's like I'm on the verge of discovering a whole new side of myself."

His words resonate with me, painting a picture of a man caught between different worlds, trying to find where he truly belongs. "It must be an overwhelming experience, rediscovering your past like this," I say, trying to offer comfort.

"It is, but it's also exciting. It's not just about finding out where I come from, but also thinking about where I'm going, and that," he says, turning to me with a meaningful look, "Includes envisioning a future with you, Naomi."

The conversation naturally flows into our shared visions of the future "I've always seen myself building a life around a family," Carson says thoughtfully. "A home filled with love, laughter, and maybe a couple of kids running around."

I smile, feeling my heart swell with affection and hope. "I can see that too. A family, and a home where everyone feels welcome and loved."

We delve into more details, our conversation meandering through various aspects of our future life together. "What about pets?" I ask, half-teasing.

Carson laughs. "Definitely. Maybe a dog? Something big and friendly that the kids can grow up with."

The idea warms me, painting a beautiful picture of a future filled with the simple joys of family life. "I'd like that, and I hope Magdalena will approve." I look around for her, but she's hiding again. She hasn't warmed to Carson yet, but I'm sure she will. "A dog, a cat, a cozy home, a family, and our diner thriving and being a central part of this community we both love."

The idea of our shared future, filled with love and laughter, creates an atmosphere of warmth and intimacy in my apartment. Carson and I continue to chat, each topic weaving a more detailed picture of the life we envision together.

"I've always imagined raising a family in a place filled with warmth and understanding," I say, leaning closer to him. "A place where our kids feel free to be themselves, to grow and explore."

Carson nods, his eyes reflecting the same dream. "Absolutely. A home where they can feel safe and loved. Where they know that no matter what, they have a place where they belong."

We talk about the kind of parents we'd like to be. Carson shares his thoughts, his voice tinged with earnestness. "I want to be the kind of dad who's there for every important moment, who supports and encourages. I never want my kids to feel that gap I felt growing up."

"I feel the same. I want to provide a nurturing environment, where they can learn and grow, and I want them to see a strong, loving relationship between us, to know what a healthy partnership looks like," I say.

As the evening progresses, our conversation shifts to the diner, our joint venture that started it all. "I see the diner not just as a business, but as an extension of our home," I say, picturing the cozy space on which we've been working. "A place where the community gathers, and where people feel connected."

Carson's hand finds mine, his grip firm and reassuring. "And I see it as a reflection of us, of our values and dreams. It's more than just a place to eat. It's a place where memories are made, where stories are shared."

The conversation is effortless, yet profound, filled with laughter and deep contemplation. We talk about everything from the color schemes for the diner to the names we might one day give our children. As the night deepens, I feel a sense of completeness. Sitting here with Carson, discussing our future, I realize how much he means to me. He's not just my partner in business. He's my partner in life, my confidant, and my support.

Finally, as the time gets close to midnight, Carson stands and pulls me into his arms. "Thank you for tonight. For sharing your dreams with me. It's nights like these that remind me of how lucky I am to have you in my life."

I wrap my arms around him, resting my head against his chest. "I'm the lucky one. To have someone who shares my dreams, who stands by me through everything. I can't wait to see what the future holds for us."

We stand there for a moment, holding each other, basking in the comfort of our shared dreams and hopes. It's a perfect ending to a night filled with love, understanding, and a deep connection that will only continue to grow.

21

A STUNNING PROPOSAL – CARSON

The crisp morning air fills my lungs as I stand outside the small café where I agreed to meet my brothers. The envelope in my pocket feels heavier than it should, laden with the potential to change our lives. I take a deep breath and step inside.

Luke, Wyatt, and Raylan are already there, their expressions a mix of apprehension and curiosity. We exchange terse greetings, the weight of the moment hanging between us.

I slide into the booth, the envelope now on the table, a silent centerpiece to our gathering. "Well, here it is," I say, my voice steady but my hands betraying a slight tremor.

Luke nods, his jaw set. "Let's hear it then."

I carefully tear open the envelope, pulling out the contents. The paper feels thin, almost fragile, in my hands. I clear my throat and start reading the results, my voice echoing slightly in the quiet café.

"As per the DNA analysis, it is confirmed that Carson Wells shares a biological relationship with the Whitmore brothers—Luke, Wyatt, and Raylan."

A heavy silence follows my words. I look up, searching their faces for reactions. Raylan is the first to break the silence, his voice barely above a whisper. "So, you're really our brother."

Wyatt leans back, a cautious smile tugging at his lips. "Guess we're a bigger family than we thought."

Luke, who had been the most skeptical, looks at the paper and then at me, his expression unreadable. Finally, he speaks. "I'll be damned. Welcome to the family, Carson."

The tension that had been building seems to dissipate, replaced by a newfound sense of connection. "I... Thank you," I manage to say, overwhelmed by the acceptance in their voices.

We spend the next hour talking, not just about the DNA results, but about our lives, our experiences, and our hopes. It's awkward at times, the years of separation evident, but there's an underlying current of eagerness, of a desire to bridge the gap that time and circumstance had created.

As we part ways, Luke claps me on the back. "We have a lot of catching up to do, brother."

Wyatt smiles. "Yeah, let's not be strangers anymore."

Raylan, still somewhat reserved, nods in agreement. "See you around, Carson."

I watch them leave, a sense of belonging slowly seeping into me. This moment, this confirmation of our shared blood, is more than just a scientific fact. It's a doorway to a family I never knew I had, and a chance to fill in the missing pieces of my life.

As I step out of the café, the sun seems to shine a little brighter, the world a little more welcoming. I have a family, brothers who accept me. It's a new beginning, a new chapter in the story of my life, and I can't wait to see where it leads.

ON THE LAST night of the renovation, Naomi and I stand in the heart of the diner, surrounded by the culmination of our hard work. The new decor blends seamlessly with the vintage charm, creating a space that's both welcoming and fresh. Tomorrow is the grand reopening, a day we've both been anticipating with a mix of excitement and nerves.

Naomi turns to me, a soft smile playing on her lips, "Can you believe it, Carson? Look at what we've created together."

I take a moment to really look around, pride swelling in my chest. "It's more than I ever imagined. It's perfect."

She walks over to the new counter, running her hand along the polished surface. "I'm a little nervous about tomorrow. It's a big day for us and for the diner."

I join her, placing my hand over hers. "It's normal to be nervous, but you're incredible. This place is a reflection of your vision and your heart. People are going to love it."

She leans into me, her head resting against my shoulder. "I couldn't have done it without you. You've been my rock through all this. I hope everyone sees how much you've contributed."

I wrap my arm around her, pulling her close. "We did this together. It's our shared dream, and regardless of what happens tomorrow, I'm just grateful to be on this journey with you."

As we stand there in our diner, I think about the journey that led us here. The ups and downs, the challenges and triumphs that have all woven the fabric of our relationship, making it stronger.

She looks up at me, her eyes shining with emotion. "After the reopening, let's take a moment for ourselves, maybe a little celebration, just the two of us."

I nod, liking the sound of that. "I'd love that. A celebration of our success, our partnership, and our future."

We spend a few more moments in the diner, taking in every detail and every memory that brought us to this point. It feels like the brink of a new chapter, not just for the diner but for us.

As we lock up, I'm filled with anticipation for what tomorrow will bring. The diner is ready, our hearts are full, and our future is bright. Together, we're about to embark on a new adventure, and I wouldn't want anyone else by my side.

THE DAY of the grand reopening dawns bright and clear, infusing Branson with a sense of celebration and anticipation. Naomi and I arrive early at the diner, the butterflies in our stomachs a mixture of nervous energy and excitement. We've put so much into this place, and now it's time to share it with the world.

As the clock strikes the opening hour, the first guests begin to trickle in, their expressions turning to awe as they take in the transformation. The new decor, a harmonious blend of vintage and modern, receives numerous compliments, filling us with a growing sense of pride and relief.

The diner quickly fills up, buzzing with the sound of lively conversations and clinking cutlery. Naomi and I move through the crowd, greeting patrons and ensuring everything runs smoothly. Amidst the hustle, I catch glimpses of her laughing and chatting with the guests, her joy infectious and heartwarming.

Just as we begin to relax into the flow of the event, a familiar figure appears at the entrance. Mr. Jenkins, who had previously caused us much distress with his drunken outbursts and possibly vandalizing of the diner, stands soberly at the threshold. Naomi and I exchange a worried glance, but we watch as he approaches us with an unexpected demeanor.

He seems steady on his feet and is neat and tidy, without the reek of alcohol as he gets near. "Carson, Naomi, I... I want to apologize," he says, his voice steady but laced with emotion. "I've realized the harm my words and actions have caused, especially to you, Carson." He looks down, then back up at us with a sincerity I hadn't seen in him before. "My comments about you were careless and hurtful. I've started attending AA meetings again, trying to turn things around."

He turns to Naomi. "I owe you a big apology too. I'm the one who broke your window and wrote the mean words for your boyfriend on the diner. I'm ashamed of myself, and I'll do what I can to pay you back. I don't have much money, but I can work...or you can tell Sheriff Bigsby." He hangs his head. "I have that coming."

The honesty in his voice and the remorse in his eyes take me by surprise. I find myself softening, appreciating the effort it must have taken for him to come here and make amends.

"Thank you, Mr. Jenkins. That means a lot," I say, extending a hand. He shakes it, a gesture of mutual respect and forgiveness.

Naomi smiles gently at him. "We appreciate your apology, Mr. Jenkins. It's good to see you taking steps toward a positive change, and when you're up for it, I could certainly use some help around here."

He nods, a small smile appearing on his face. "I wish you both the best with the diner. It looks wonderful."

With that, he turns and leaves, allowing us to breathe a sigh of relief. The weight of his previous actions seems to lift, leaving room for a newfound sense of peace.

"I knew it must be him, but the sheriff had no proof." Naomi sighs. "I feel much better now that I know for sure, and I hope he can really turn things around."

"So do I." I care a surprising amount about the man, considering he was always hostile to me before, and he trashed the diner because he was angry at me for whatever reason he blew up in his mind during a drunken binge.

The rest of the day passes in a blur of celebration. The diner is alive with energy, laughter, and the clinking of glasses. Naomi and I steal moments together, sharing smiles and quiet words of gratitude. The success of the reopening feels sweeter in the light of overcoming past hurdles.

As the day turns into evening, and the last guests leave, we find ourselves alone in the diner, standing amidst the remnants of our successful day. We wrap our arms around each other, a sense of accomplishment and contentment enveloping us.

"We did it," I whisper, feeling her warmth against me.

"We really did," she says, her voice filled with happiness. "And we did it together."

In the quiet aftermath of the grand reopening, the diner transforms into a stage set for a more intimate celebration. We stand in the heart of the space we've lovingly brought back to life, surrounded by echoes of laughter and shared achievement.

As I reach into my pocket, my fingers fumble nervously around the small box that holds a symbol of my commitment. The air feels thick with anticipation, a stark contrast to the easy banter of the day's festivities. I turn to face

Naomi, her eyes reflecting the soft light, unaware of the life-changing moment I'm about to initiate.

"Naomi," I say, my voice trembling slightly, "Today has been a dream come true in so many ways, but there's one more thing I want to do to make it absolutely perfect."

Her smile is curious and expectant. I take a deep breath, attempting to steady my nerves. As I drop to one knee, the ring box feels slippery in my moist palm. In a moment of clumsiness, my fingers, slick with nervous sweat, fumble, and the box slips, clattering to the floor. We both freeze, and then burst into laughter, the sound echoing warmly around us.

"Sorry." I chuckle, red-faced as I quickly scoop up the box. "I guess I'm more nervous than I thought."

Naomi's laughter is a melody that eases my jitters. I finally manage to open the box, revealing the ring. It's a vintage piece, its design echoing the locket I gave her, and symbolizing the merging of our pasts into a shared future.

Her laughter fades into a soft gasp. "Carson, it's beautiful," she whispers.

I take her hand, steadier now. "Naomi, you've filled my life with laughter, love, and a sense of belonging I've never known before. With you, every day is a new adventure, and a chapter in the best story ever told. I love you more than words can express, and I want to continue writing this story with you, forever. Will you marry me?"

Tears brim in her eyes, shining like the ring itself. For a heartbeat, the world stands still. Then she nods vigorously, her voice a mix of laughter and tears. "Yes, Carson, a million times yes."

Relieved, I carefully slide the ring onto her finger, its presence a tangible symbol of our love and commitment. I stand up and take her into my arms, our embrace a cocoon of love, sealing our promise to each other.

As we pull back, her eyes dance with happiness. "I can't believe you dropped the ring," she teases, her smile radiant.

I join in her laughter, my heart light and full. "I guess that just makes it a more memorable proposal."

The diner, once a backdrop for our professional collaboration, has now witnessed the most personal and significant moment of our lives. Hand in hand, we step out into the starlit night, our hearts full of love, joy, and anticipation for the life we will build together.

22

STRONGER TOGETHER – NAOMI

The diner is closed on Monday, a rare pause in our bustling routine. It gives me the perfect opportunity to catch up with Jenny and Fallon. We agree to meet for lunch at a quaint café downtown, a spot we've always loved for its cozy atmosphere and great food.

I arrive a bit early, the engagement ring on my finger feeling like a beacon of the new chapter in my life. As I wait, I can't help but admire the ring, each glance a reminder of Carson's love and our shared dreams.

Jenny and Fallon arrive together, their smiles turning to gasps of surprise as they notice the ring. "Oh my gosh, Naomi. Is that what I think it is?" asks Fallon, her eyes wide.

A huge smile stretches my cheeks as I extend my hand for them to see. "Yes, Carson proposed on the night of the reopening."

They both lean in, inspecting the ring, their expressions a mix of awe and excitement. "It's gorgeous, Naomi. I'm so happy for you both," says Jenny says, her initial surprise turning into a warm smile. "I can't believe I didn't notice the ring before."

I put a hand over it reflexively. "I wear it on a chain while working, so I don't lose or damage it."

Fallon hugs me tightly, her joy infectious. "This is amazing news. You two are perfect for each other."

As we settle into our seats and order lunch, the conversation naturally revolves around the proposal. I recount the story, and their laughter mingles with mine at the mention of Carson dropping the ring.

During a lull in conversation, Jenny gives me a gentle, concerned look. "I'm really happy for you, but aren't you worried things are moving a bit fast?"

Her question gives me a moment's pause. "I've thought about that, but with Carson, it just feels right. We've been through a lot together already, and it's only made us stronger."

She nods, her expression softening. "I trust your judgment. You've always been level-headed about these things. Just promise you'll take the time you both need to make sure it's right."

I appreciate her concern, touched by her care for my well-being. "I promise, Jenny. We're taking this step together, fully aware of what it means for both of us."

The conversation shifts to the diner and its resurgence in popularity, the likes of which I've never seen. "It's amazing how well you two work together," says Fallon. "The diner's never been better."

I smile, thinking of the countless hours and decisions shared with Carson. "It's been a journey, but we're a great team. We complement each other in so many ways."

As lunch comes to an end, we part ways with hugs and promises to catch up again soon. As I walk back to my car, my heart feels full. Despite the challenges and changes ahead, Carson and I are stronger together, and no obstacle can change the love and commitment we share.

After our lunch, I drive to Table Rock Lake, where Carson is waiting for me. The autumn sun casts a golden glow over the water, creating a serene backdrop for our afternoon together. Despite the busy schedule of the diner, moments like these are vital—a reminder of the simple joys we share.

I find him by the docks near the Chateau On The Lake. He's already rented a small boat equipped with fishing gear. His smile is as warm as the sunlight when he sees me. "Ready for a little adventure on the lake?" he asks, his eyes twinkling with excitement.

I laugh, a sense of freedom washing over me. "Absolutely. Let's see if we can catch our dinner."

As we set out on the water, the gentle rocking of the boat and the quiet surroundings create a peaceful ambiance. The boat gently glides away from the dock, carrying us into the heart of Table Rock Lake's serene waters. Carson handles the boat with a confidence that matches his smile.

"You know, I might need a refresher on fishing," I tease, watching him prepare the fishing rods. "Then again, I might surprise you with my skills."

Carson laughs, a sound that blends perfectly with the soft lapping of the water against our boat. "Is that a challenge? Because you should know, I'm pretty handy with a fishing rod myself."

The playful banter sets the tone for our afternoon. We each cast our lines, the silence of the moment broken only by our occasional laughter and the distant calls of birds.

"So, who do you think will catch the first fish?" I ask, watching the bobber on my line dance lightly on the water's surface.

Carson glances at me, a mock-serious look on his face. "Considering my vast fishing experience since Ted liked to fish every weekend, I'd say the odds are in my favor."

I roll my eyes playfully. "Vast experience, huh? We'll see about that. My dad and brothers also fished on weekends, and I tagged along a lot."

Time seems to stand still as we wait for a bite, the tranquility of the lake enveloping us. I lose myself in the beauty of the moment, the peacefulness of the water, and the warmth of the sun on my skin.

Suddenly, his rod jerks, signaling a catch. "Looks like I've got something." He focuses on reeling it in with determination.

I watch, amused and impressed, as he skillfully brings in a decent-sized fish. "Okay, I'll give you that one. Nice catch."

He grins, holding up his prize. "One-nil, Naomi. Let's see what you've got."

Not long after, my own line gives a telltale tug. "Looks like it's my turn," I say, excitement bubbling within me. I reel in, feeling the weight of the fish fighting against me. With a bit of effort and a lot of cheering from Carson, I finally bring in my catch. "Looks like we're even now."

He squints. "Mine's an inch longer."

"An inch isn't anything to brag about, love."

Our joint laughter echoes across the lake, the joy of the moment shared in our small boat. We continue fishing, talking, and enjoying each other's company, the hours slipping by unnoticed.

As the sun begins to dip toward the horizon, casting a warm, golden light over everything, he turns to me, his expression softening.

"I love days like these. No matter where life takes us, these moments are what keep me grounded."

I lean closer to him, feeling a surge of affection. "I feel the same. It's the simple things that mean everything."

The gentle sway of the boat on Table Rock Lake's tranquil waters creates a serene backdrop, perfect for the kind of heart-to-heart talks that have become a cornerstone of my relationship with Carson. As he maneuvers the boat with a practiced ease, his smile warms me more than the soft glow of the setting sun.

I sit across from him, our fishing lines bobbing in the calm lake, the playful competition from earlier still lingering in the air. "You know, I had almost forgotten how peaceful it can be out here," I say, taking in the sprawling beauty of the lake. "I haven't been out here since my dad died, and I got older. My brothers are off living their lives..." I sigh heavily. "It's normal but a little sad when I think about it."

Carson nods, his eyes reflecting the golden hues of the sunset. "It's moments like these that remind us to slow down and appreciate the time we have with special people."

Our conversation meanders through light topics, laughter interspersed with comfortable silences, but as the sun begins its descent, painting the sky in shades of orange and pink, his demeanor shifts. There's a seriousness in his eyes that piques my curiosity.

"Naomi," he says, his voice carrying a weight that instantly captures my attention. "I need to talk to you about something important."

I lean in, my playful mood replaced by concern. "What's going on?" Surely, he doesn't have more doubts about us.

He takes a deep breath, his gaze lingering on the horizon before meeting mine. "I have to go back to Texas for a while. There are some things I need to take care of—business matters and personal stuff. It's important."

The news hits me like a sudden change in the wind. His words send a swirl of emotions through me, a mixture of understanding and a tinge of sadness. Realizing Carson will be tying up loose ends in Texas to fully commit to a life here in Branson with me brings a hopeful flutter to my heart. That must be his reason for going back to Texax since he's integrated himself into the diner and our life here.

"How long do you think you'll be gone?" I ask, trying to mask the melancholy in my voice. I don't want to be parted from him, but I understand the reason.

He looks out over the lake, the fading light casting shadows on his face. "I'm not exactly sure. A few weeks, but maybe more. There are a lot of things I need to sort out."

The thought of being apart for that long feels daunting, but I understand the necessity of his journey. "I wish I could come with you," I say, a part of me longing to throw aside caution and go with him despite my responsibilities.

Carson's gaze meets mine, filled with a mixture of longing and resignation. "I wish that too, but the diner needs you right now, especially after the reopening. It wouldn't be right to ask you to leave it."

I nod, feeling a sense of pride in the responsibility I hold. "The diner is a big part of who I am, but so are you. We'll make it work, no matter the distance."

We spend the rest of the evening in a blend of conversation and contemplative silence, enjoying the peaceful setting and each other's company. The simple act of fishing, the rhythm of the water, the shared smiles, and touches all feel bittersweet, knowing soon we'll be so far apart.

As the sun dips below the horizon, leaving a trail of fiery colors across the sky, we pack up our gear and head back to shore. The air is cooler now, a gentle reminder of the changing seasons and the transitions in our own lives.

He turns to me, a soft smile on his lips. "Do you want to stay at the hotel with me tonight? It's closer, and we could make the most of the time we have left."

I hesitate for a moment, thinking of the diner, and the endless to-do list that awaits me, but the thought of spending another night with Carson, especially now, feels too precious to pass up. "Yes, I'd like that," I say, the decision bringing a sense of relief and excitement.

The walk back to the Chateau On The Lake is short, but it feels different this time, more poignant. We talk about little things, the day's catch, and the beauty of the lake, but there's an underlying current of emotion that neither of us can ignore.

Once at the hotel, we head to his room, a comfortable space that's become a familiar haven over the past few weeks. The room is dimly lit, the soft glow of the bedside lamps casting a warm ambiance. We sit on the edge of the bed, side by side, our hands intertwined.

"I'm going to miss this," he says, his voice low. "Miss waking up to you, miss our coffee chats in the morning, our morning showers, and the late-night loving."

I lean my head on his shoulder, feeling the steady rhythm of his heartbeat. "We'll have plenty more times like that. This is just a short break."

He wraps an arm around me, pulling me closer. "I know. It's just hard to leave, knowing how much I'm going to miss you."

We sit there for a while, lost in our thoughts, savoring the closeness. The night deepens around us, the soft hum of the hotel creating a cocoon that shields us from the world outside.

Eventually, we lie down, the bed enveloping us in its comfort. Our conversation drifts to future plans, to dreams of what we'll do when he returns. The talk is light but filled with hope and anticipation.

As sleep begins to claim us, Carson's lips press gently against my forehead. "Good night, Naomi," he whispers.

"Good night, Carson," I say, my heart full despite the looming goodbye. We fall asleep in each other's arms, the bond between us a strong tether that will hold us together through the days apart.

23

PARTING IS SWEET SORROW – CARSON

The early morning sun casts a warm glow over the diner as I pull into the parking lot. Today is the day I leave for Texas, and the thought of parting with Naomi fills me with a bittersweet ache. I take a deep breath, steeling myself for the goodbye, and step out of the car.

Naomi is already there, waiting for me. Her smile is brave, but her eyes betray the sadness we both feel. We walk into the diner together, the place where our journey began, and now the setting for our temporary farewell.

"I'll miss this," I say, gesturing to the diner, "And you, most of all."

She nods, her hand finding mine. "I'll miss you too. This place won't be the same without you."

We're interrupted by the sound of a car pulling up. It's my brothers, Luke, Wyatt, and Raylan, coming to see me off. Their presence adds a layer of family warmth to the farewell.

"Couldn't let you leave without a proper send-off, brother," says Luke with a grin, clapping me on the back.

Luke's easygoing demeanor and clear acceptance of our being related brings a lightness to the moment, his grin infectious as he pulls me into a brotherly hug. Wyatt and Raylan follow suit, their handshakes firm, and their smiles genuine.

"So, Texas, huh?" Wyatt remarks, leaning against a counter. "Gonna bring back some of that Lone Star charm to Branson?"

I chuckle, glancing at Naomi. "Soon, I hope. I've got a bit of business to settle, but I'll be back. Branson's become a second home to me."

Raylan, who's been quietly observing, says, "Just make sure you come back. We're just starting to get used to having another brother around."

The warmth and acceptance in their words are more comforting than I can express. I find myself feeling grateful for this newfound connection with my brothers.

Naomi smiles at their banter, her presence a reassuring constant beside me. "Don't worry. I'll make sure he comes back. We've got a lot of plans for the diner."

"Speaking of which," says Luke, glancing around, "You two have done a great job with the place. It's good to see it thriving."

The conversation flows naturally, filled with light-hearted jokes and updates on family news. Naomi and my brothers interact with an ease that warms my heart. It's a glimpse of the future I hope for—one where my life in Texas and my life in Branson seamlessly intertwine.

As the time for my departure draws near, a lump forms in my throat. I turn to Naomi, her gaze meeting mine with a mixture of love and sadness. "I'll be thinking of you every day," I say, my voice thick with emotion.

"I'll miss you too." Her hand squeezes mine. "Be safe,

Carson, and remember, this is just a 'see you later,' not a goodbye."

We share a final embrace, a promise of our commitment and the future we're building together. As I pull away, my brothers give me a collective nod, a silent assurance of their support.

With a heavy heart, I step outside the diner, the familiar chime of the bell ringing out as I leave. I take one last look back, memorizing the scene—Naomi standing with my brothers, a symbol of the new life I've found here, and the promise of the future before us.

As I drive to the regional airport, the memories of the past few weeks play through my mind. Naomi, the diner, and my brothers have all become integral parts of my life. No matter what happens in Texas, my path will lead me back to Branson, and back to them.

This isn't an end, just a pause in the beautiful journey that lies ahead, and with that thought, I find the strength to face the upcoming weeks, knowing that a bright future awaits us all.

RETURNING TO TEXAS, the sprawling expanse of my house greets me with an eerie silence, starkly contrasting the cozy bustle of Naomi's diner. The walls, adorned with artwork and memories of solo travels, now seem to mock my solitude. I drift through the rooms, each step echoing in the hollow space, a constant reminder of Naomi's absence.

In Branson, every moment was filled with purpose and partnership. Here, in the vastness of my home, I find myself listlessly wandering from room to room, Naomi's laughter and the warmth of our shared life haunting my thoughts.

My bed feels too large and empty, the dinners too quiet and solitary. The joy and contentment I found in our simple shared routines now replaced by a void that echoes through the luxurious but lonely halls of my house.

At work, as a real estate developer, I struggle to focus. Projects that once commanded my full attention now seem trivial in comparison to the life I've left behind. My team's questions are met with distracted responses, my gaze often drifting out the window, lost in memories of recent days spent with Naomi. The once satisfying clatter of development and progress now feels jarringly empty.

This dissonance reaches a peak one morning when Ellen calls. Her voice, warm and concerned, is a lifeline in my sea of distraction. "Carson, dear, let's have lunch. You sound like you could use some company."

Grateful for the offer, I agree to meet her at our favorite restaurant, a place that has always felt like an extension of home. As I sit across from Ellen a couple of hours later, her perceptive gaze quickly notices my unease.

"You're miles away, Carson. What's on your mind?" she asks, her voice laced with concern.

I try to smile, but it feels forced. "It's Naomi. I didn't realize how much being away from her would affect me. This house, my work...it all feels empty without her."

She reaches across the table, her hand warm and reassuring. "You've found something special. It's natural to feel this way. Home isn't a place so much as it's where your heart is."

Her words strike a chord, and I find myself pouring out my feelings, my doubts, and my plans for the future with Naomi. She listens intently, offering nods of understanding and words of wisdom.

"Focus on what matters. You have a chance at a life filled

with love and partnership. Don't let the distance cloud your judgment. Finish your work here, but keep your heart focused on what you truly want."

Her patient gaze encourages me to delve deeper into my thoughts, the conflict within me becoming clearer as I speak. "I'm torn. Ted entrusted his business to me, and I've continued to expand it. It's a part of me, yet it anchors me here. I can't just uproot and run it from Branson."

She nods, her eyes reflecting a deep understanding. "It's a difficult situation, but sometimes, life requires us to make tough decisions. It's about prioritizing what truly matters."

I take a sip of my coffee, feeling the weight of her words. "I know. That's why I'm trying to restructure things here, to give myself the freedom to spend more time in Branson. I want to help Naomi transition, to start our life together, but I also need to ensure my business here is secure."

She leans back, her expression thoughtful. "It sounds like you're planning for a future with Naomi in Texas. Have you discussed this with her?"

I pause, realizing the gravity of what that entails. "Not in so many words. We've talked about our future, but I haven't specifically mentioned moving her to Texas. I guess I just assumed..."

Her gentle interruption steers me back to reality. "Assumptions can be dangerous. It's crucial to have these conversations openly. Naomi's life is in Branson, along with her diner and community. Moving to Texas would be a significant change for her."

The complexity of the situation dawns on me, and I feel a pang of uncertainty. "You're right, Ellen. I need to talk to Naomi about this, to really understand what she wants, what we both want." Surely, she must realize she has to move to Texas after we're married? How can she imagine otherwise?

The rest of our lunch is spent discussing various aspects of balancing personal life with professional responsibilities. Ellen's advice, as always, is invaluable—a mix of wisdom and practicality.

As I leave the restaurant, my mind is abuzz with thoughts and plans. The drive back to my office is a contemplative one, each mile a reminder of the distance between Naomi and me. It seems obvious that our future is in Texas, but I'm nervous that she hasn't reached the same conclusion. I'm suddenly impatient to discuss it with her, but it seems like the kind of conversation we should have face-to-face.

24

HOMECOMING – NAOMI

Carson returns from Texas after several weeks away. He's been busy settling his affairs there and getting ready to move back to Branson permanently. I'm eager to see him, to show him how much I've missed him.

I hear a car pull up outside my apartment and hurry to the door, opening it before he can knock. He stands on the porch, a bouquet of flowers in one hand and a bottle of wine in the other. His eyes meet mine, and my pulse quickens.

"Hi," he says softly, stepping inside and closing the door behind him.

"Hi, yourself." I smile, taking the flowers and wine from him. "These are beautiful."

His gaze lingers on me, sending shivers down my spine. "Not nearly as beautiful as you."

I blush, feeling a flutter of anticipation as I lead him inside. The air is charged with electric energy, and I wonder if he feels it too. I set the flowers and wine on the kitchen counter, turning to face him.

He steps closer, cupping my cheek in his hand. "I've missed you so much."

My breath catches in my throat as his lips brush against mine. His touch is like fire, igniting a burning desire within me. I lean into him, savoring the taste of his kiss. He pulls me close, and I melt into him, my body responding to his every movement. We lose ourselves in the moment, our passion fueled by the weeks of separation.

We only break apart, breathless and flushed, because the oven timer sounds. "That's the bread," I say, reluctantly pulling away.

"Let me help," he offers.

I nod, and we work side by side, preparing the meal. The familiar routine is comforting, yet I feel a new energy between us, a deeper connection, as if the distance has made us appreciate each other even more.

"It smells delicious," he says, as I add the finishing touches to the pasta sauce. He steps closer, wrapping his arms around my waist and resting his chin on my shoulder. I lean back into him, savoring the closeness.

"I'm glad you're here," I whisper, my voice thick with emotion.

"Me too." He gently kisses my neck. The sensation sends a shiver down my spine, and I turn to face him, our eyes locking in an intense gaze. The air crackles with electricity, and he leans in, capturing my lips in a searing kiss that leaves me breathless.

As we break apart, I smile at him, my heart full of love and happiness. "Let's eat," I say, gesturing to the pasta dish I've prepared.

We sit down to enjoy the meal, chatting amiably about the diner's progress and the town's response to the renovations. "Business is booming. I might need to hire another server."

He smiles, nodding. "It's great to see the community embracing the changes. The fusion menu was a good idea."

I take a bite of my food, savoring the rich flavor as I mull over his words. "I'm glad everyone likes it. I was worried at first, but it's been a hit."

He reaches over, squeezing my hand reassuringly. "You did an amazing job. This place is thriving, and it's all thanks to you."

His praise warms my heart, and I smile at him. "It's all thanks to us. You've been such a huge part of this. I couldn't have done it without you."

He grins, leaning in for a quick kiss. "We're a pretty great team, aren't we?"

I nod, my eyes sparkling with happiness. "The best."

We finish our meals and wash the dishes together. The entire time, a heavy sensuality hangs between us. It's been weeks since we were intimate, and I can't wait much longer.

After cleaning up, I turn to him, my gaze smoldering. "I want you, Carson."

His eyes darken with desire, and he pulls me close, his lips crashing down on mine. Our kisses grow more urgent, and soon we're tearing at each other's clothes, desperate for skin-to-skin contact. We stumble through the house, our bodies entwined, until we reach the bedroom.

I tug at his shirt, and he helps me remove it, exposing the toned muscles of his chest and abdomen. I run my hands over his bare skin, reveling in the feel of him beneath my fingertips as he undresses me slowly, teasingly.

I gasp as his fingers brush across my sensitive nipples, sending shivers of pleasure down my spine. He lowers his head, capturing one nipple in his mouth and sucking gently, eliciting a moan of pleasure from my lips while I slip my hand into his waistband, stroking his hard length.

He groans, pressing himself against my palm, and I can feel the heat radiating from his body. I unbuckle his belt, pushing his pants and underwear down his hips, freeing his cock. He kicks off his remaining clothing, and we stand naked before each other, our eyes locked in a heated gaze.

The air is thick with desire as he guides me onto the bed, his hands moving slowly over my body, exploring every curve and valley. I arch into his touch, my skin tingling with anticipation as he trails kisses down my neck, his tongue tracing a path along my collarbone.

His lips continue their descent, brushing across the swell of my breasts before capturing one nipple between them, sucking and teasing the sensitive bud. I writhe beneath him, my body aching for more as he continues his exploration, his fingers finding their way between my legs while his mouth lavishes attention on my other breast.

I gasp as he slides two fingers inside me, curling them in a way that makes me see stars. He strokes me with expert precision, driving his fingers in and out of my slick heat while his thumb circles my clit, sending waves of pleasure coursing through my veins.

I reach down, grasping his cock in my hand and stroking him in time with the rhythm of his thrusts. He groans, his eyes fluttering shut as I run my thumb over the tip, spreading the bead of moisture gathered there.

"That feels so good," he says, his voice husky with desire.

I increase my pace, matching the tempo of his fingers buried inside me. The pressure builds within me, a coil of tension winding tighter and tighter until it snaps, sending me spiraling into ecstasy. My orgasm crashes through me, wave after wave of pleasure washing over my body as I cry out in release. Carson follows soon after as I tighten my grip on him, stroking him to completion.

We lie spent in each other's arms, our breathing ragged, and our bodies slick with sweat. I rest my head on his chest, listening to the steady beat of his heart. I lift my head when he exhales. "Something wrong?"

He shakes his head. "No. That just went differently than I planned. I wanted to be inside you."

I smile, gently stroking his softened cock. "We have all night."

His eyes darken with desire as he pulls me closer, his lips capturing mine in a searing kiss. I melt into him, losing myself in the delicious sensation of his body pressed against mine. My desire surges again, and his cock is starting to harden against my hand.

I break the kiss, gazing up at him. "I need you inside me."

He groans, rolling us over so I'm on top of him. "Ride me, baby."

I straddle him, reaching over to grab a condom from the nightstand drawer. I roll it on, positioning myself above his shaft. He grips my hips, guiding me down onto his cock. I gasp as he fills me, stretching me in the most delicious way.

I start to move, rocking my hips as I ride him. He thrusts upward, meeting my movements with his own. His hands grip my waist, holding me steady as I grind against him. Our gazes lock, and I see nothing but love and desire in his eyes.

I lean down, capturing his lips in a searing kiss as we move together, our bodies in perfect sync. The tension builds within me, coiling tighter and tighter until I can't hold back anymore. I sit up again, squeezing my thighs around his legs as I chase my release.

He reaches between us, rubbing my clit in slow, deliberate circles. The added stimulation pushes me over the edge, and I cry out as I come, my body shuddering with pleasure. I can't look away from his brown eyes, the love in them intensifying my orgasm.

As I come down from my high, he flips us over, so I'm lying on my back. He thrusts into me again, his pace faster now. I wrap my legs around his waist, urging him on. He kisses me, swallowing my moans of pleasure as he drives into me. His rhythm grows erratic, and I know he's close.

I reach down, gripping his ass and pulling him closer. Carson tenses, groaning as he comes, his cock pulsing inside me as he spills his seed. We collapse in a heap of tangled limbs, our hearts beating in unison.

"I love you," I whisper, stroking his hair.

"I love you too." He smiles, kissing me tenderly.

We lay there for a while, basking in the afterglow. Eventually, we get up and shower together, enjoying the closeness. As we're soaping up, I ask, "How was your trip? We barely talked about it." I flush, realizing most of our conversation centered on the diner and how much we missed each other.

He chuckles, rinsing off before stepping out of the shower. "It was good. I got everything squared away so I can stay here long enough to help you find a manager and organize your affairs for the move."

Shampoo is in my eyes as I blink at him. I hastily duck under the stream and finish rinsing before stepping out as well. "What do you mean?"

"I think three months is doable to get everything tied up here before we go to Texas. Do you think it'll take longer than that to hire a manager and sort through things and pack?" He looks doubtful.

My mouth drops open. "Go to Texas? For a visit?" Maybe

he wants me to meet his stepgran, but I have a sinking sensation as I look into his puzzled gaze.

"Not for a visit. To live." His brow furrows. "I thought you understood."

"Understood what?" I stare at him, my mind racing.

"That once we're married, we'd be living in Texas. My life is there, with Ellen and my company. I can't just abandon everything."

I shake my head, my heart pounding as his words sink in. "But you said you wanted to be part of this community. You want to invest in the diner and build our lives together here."

He sighs, running a hand through his hair. "I do, but I have obligations back home. I can't just walk away from my responsibilities, and I never said I wanted to build our lives here. I plan to visit frequently to get to know my brothers better, and I assumed you'd want to come back every few months to check in on the diner too."

"So, you expect me to just give up everything I've worked for and follow you to Texas?" I stare at him, incredulous.

His eyes flash with anger. "I'm not asking you to give up anything. I'm offering you a better life in a bigger city, where you can expand your horizons. It's a lot easier for you to leave your diner than it is for me to leave my conglomerate."

I glare at him. "Why can't you hire a manager, since that's what you expect me to do?"

He sighs, raking a hand through his hair. "Because that's not how my business works. I need to be involved in every aspect of it, and that's not possible if I'm living here." He shakes his head. "I'm talking about a multi-million-dollar company. Your diner can't compare to that."

His words sting, and I step back, stung. "So, I'm not worth as much as your business?"

"That's not what I meant." He reaches for me, but I pull away.

"Then what did you mean?" I demand, crossing my arms over my chest.

"I meant that my life is in Texas. I can't just uproot everything and move here permanently." He looks frustrated. "I guess I thought you'd understand that. I should have stated the obvious sooner. We have to live in Texas, but I have three months free to be able to help ease the transition for you. How can I help?"

"You can help by forgetting about that. I'm not leaving Branson." I square my shoulders and glare at him. "I can't believe you'd ask me to."

"And I can't believe you'd think I could leave everything in my life to settle here." He storms to the living room and jerks on his clothes. "You're being unreasonable, Naomi."

"Am I?" I cross my arms. "Or am I the only one of us thinking clearly right now?"

"Clearly?" He scoffs. "I'm trying to give you a better life, and you're refusing it. Refusing me." With that, he storms to the door, hesitating for just a second with his hand on the knob. It's like he expects me to call him back or ask him not to go.

I'm too upset and blindsided to do so. My stubborn pride keeps me silent as he swings open the door and slams it behind him a moment later. I stand there, stunned and hurt, as I replay our conversation over in my mind. Was I really being unreasonable? Or was he?

I don't know anymore. All I know is that I feel betrayed and alone. How could he keep something like that from me? And how could he expect me to just uproot my entire life for him? I can't abandon the diner, my family, and my community. I just can't.

25

COMMUNITY TIES – CARSON

The door slams shut behind me, the sound echoing my turbulent emotions. Anger, frustration, and a sense of betrayal churn within me as I stride away from Naomi's apartment. Her refusal to even consider moving to Texas feels like a rejection of everything I'm offering her—a life filled with possibilities and security. In my mind, I had already envisioned our future together, but her adamant stance to stay in Branson shatters that image.

Seeking solace, I find myself at a local bar, the dim lighting matching my somber mood. I sit at the counter, ordering a drink, my thoughts swirling around Naomi's rejection. To me, asking her to move to Texas wasn't just a logistical decision. It was an invitation to share my life and my world. Her dismissal of this feels personal, as if she's discounting the life I've built.

As I brood over my drink, contemplating the vast divide between our desires, the door opens, and in walk my brothers—Wyatt, Raylan, and Luke. They spot me at the bar and make their way over, their expressions a mix of concern and curiosity.

The clink of glasses and the low hum of conversation in the bar provide a backdrop to the impromptu family meeting unfolding. Wyatt, Raylan, and Luke pull up chairs, their faces etched with brotherly concern.

"What's going on, Carson?" Wyatt's voice cuts through my reverie. "You look like you've lost your best friend."

I exhale, feeling the weight of their collective gaze. "It's about Naomi. I asked her to move to Texas with me, and...she said no. She's adamant about staying in Branson."

Luke leans forward, his brow furrowed. "But why can't you just stay here? I mean, you've got us, the diner's going great with Naomi..."

I run a hand through my hair, the frustration evident in my tone. "It's not that simple, Luke. My life, my entire business is in Texas. I've built a real estate empire from Ted's legacy that needs my direct oversight. I can't manage that remotely, not on the scale it's grown to."

Raylan nods. "Makes sense, but have you considered Naomi's side in this? She's got her own roots in Branson, and the diner is her legacy."

Wyatt chimes in, his voice calm but firm. "Moving to Texas is a big ask. It's not just about geography. It's about her identity, and her place in our community. These ties run deep."

Their words hit home, forcing me to reconsider my stance. Naomi's connection to Branson is as integral to her as my ties are to Texas. "I get that, I really do, but how do we bridge this gap? I can't uproot my life in Texas, and she feels the same about Branson."

The conversation shifts as we brainstorm solutions, each brother offering their perspective. Luke suggests a long-distance relationship, at least for a while. "Maybe you could split your time between here and Texas? It's not ideal, but it could be a start."

Raylan adds, "And technology makes it easier to stay connected. You could work remotely part of the time, couldn't you?"

Wyatt nods in agreement. "It's about compromise. You both might have to make sacrifices, but that's what relationships are about."

Their advice begins to open my eyes to possibilities I hadn't considered. A balance between my life in Texas and my life with Naomi in Branson might be challenging, but not impossible.

As I leave the bar and make my way back to my hotel room at the Chateau On The Lake, my mind is a whirlwind of emotions and thoughts. The conversation with my brothers has introduced new avenues of thinking, yet the solution to the impasse with Naomi still feels elusive.

In the solitude of my room, I try to envision various scenarios where Naomi and I could make our relationship work despite the distance. Could I manage part of my business remotely, spending a few weeks in Branson and then a few in Texas? The idea seems feasible, but the practicalities are daunting.

I spend a mostly sleepless night, tossing and turning, trying to reconcile my desire to be with Naomi and the reality of my responsibilities in Texas. It's a tug-of-war between my heart and my obligations, and the strain is substantial.

As the first light of dawn filters through the curtains, my phone rings. It's Ellen, her voice instantly soothing, yet filled with concern. "Carson, you sound exhausted. Is everything all right?"

I prop myself up against the headboard, the phone

pressed to my ear, grateful for Ellen's voice, a familiar anchor in the storm of my thoughts. "I'm struggling," I admit, my voice reflecting the weariness I feel. "It's about Naomi and me. There's a divide between our lives in Texas and Branson, and I can't seem to bridge it."

Her response is patient and thoughtful. "Tell me everything, Carson. Sometimes, speaking it aloud can bring clarity."

Holding the phone a little tighter, I try to find the right words to express the turmoil inside me. "It's like I'm caught between two worlds. In Branson, with Naomi, I feel a sense of belonging I never knew I needed. We're building something together, something meaningful, but back in Texas, my business...it's not just a job. It's a part of who I am."

Ellen's voice is a comforting presence in the quiet room. "I understand. It sounds like you're deeply torn."

"Yes, deeply," I echo, the words resonating with my current state. "Naomi has her own life in Branson, her diner, and her community. It's her world, and she's invited me into it. I never expected to feel so connected to a place, to a person, in such a short time."

"And yet, you have responsibilities in Texas.", Her tone is understanding but probing.

"Exactly. My company, the people who depend on me, everything I've built... I can't just walk away from that, but the thought of not being with Naomi..." I trail off, the conflict clear in my voice.

She's silent for a moment, allowing the weight of my words to settle. "Love often requires us to make difficult choices, just as Amelia once faced. Have you considered what you might be willing to sacrifice, or change, for the sake of this relationship?"

Her question hits me like a wave, forcing me to confront

a reality I've been avoiding. "Sacrifice... I've worked tirelessly to get where I am, but losing Naomi seems like a loss too great to bear."

"Then perhaps it's time to think creatively," she says softly. "You've always had a knack for finding solutions where others see barriers."

"You mean, finding a way to balance my life in Texas with my life in Branson?" I ask, a flicker of hope igniting within me.

"Exactly. Life is about finding harmony between our desires and our responsibilities. I believe you have the ability to create a solution that honors both."

We talk more, exploring the possibilities and the potential compromises. Ellen's words and wisdom guide me toward a path that feels less daunting, and more hopeful. "Thank you, Ellen," I say, feeling a sense of direction emerging from our conversation. "You always have a way of cutting through the crap."

She laughs. "That's the Texan in me. Just remember, dear, don't let your apprehensions prevent you from pursuing a life full of love."

As we end the call, the light of the new day brings a renewed sense of purpose. Ellen's counsel has given me a new perspective anda resolve to find a way to weave together the disparate threads of my life in Texas and my burgeoning life with Naomi in Branson. It's time for an honest, open conversation with Naomi.

26

COMPROMISE – NAOMI

The morning sun does little to lift the gloom that has settled over me as I unlock the diner's front door. My mind is a whirlwind of hurt and anger from last night's confrontation with Carson. The clatter of pots and the hiss of the coffee machine can't drown out the echo of his words and my own feelings of betrayal.

Fallon walks in, concern etched on her face. "I heard about last night from Wyatt. Are you okay?"

I shake my head, the frustration evident in my voice. "I don't know. I just can't believe he expects me to uproot my life and move to Texas without even discussing it with me first."

She sighs, her expression sympathetic. "That's tough, but maybe there's a way to work this out? Love's about finding a middle ground, right?"

Before I can respond, Jenny joins us, her usual cheerful demeanor replaced by a look of concern. "I overheard, Naomi. It's a big decision, but maybe Carson has a point? I mean, the diner's important, but it's not the only thing in your life."

I bristle at her words, my loyalty to the diner and my community feeling like a shield against the uncertainty Carson's proposal has brought. "This diner is my legacy, Jenny. It's what I've worked for all these years. I can't just leave it."

Fallon leans against the counter, her tone gentle but firm. "But what if you didn't have to leave it behind entirely? What if you found someone you trust to manage it while you're away?"

The idea gives me pause, the thought of entrusting the diner to someone else both frightening and liberating. Carson mentioned that last night, but I wasn't ready to hear it then. Now, I can consider it more dispassionately. "I... I don't know. It feels like giving up a part of myself."

Jenny moves closer, her voice earnest. "You've built something amazing here, but it doesn't mean you can't build something new with Carson. You'd still be part of the diner, just not tied down to it every day."

Their words begin to seep through the wall of resistance I've built. Love, I realize, is about compromise, about growing and adapting, but can I really let go, even a little, of what I've built here? The conversation with Fallon and Jenny continues, their words gradually weaving through my resistance, planting seeds of possibility and compromise.

"Think about it," says Jenny, her hands animatedly expressing her thoughts. "You love this diner, sure, but don't you also love Carson? Sometimes, love means making tough choices."

Fallon nods in agreement, her voice soothing yet persuasive. "You've nurtured this place into something special, but delegating some responsibilities might actually be good for you, and for the diner too."

I chew on my lip, considering their words. "I... I'm just

scared, you know? This diner is everything I know, and Carson... I love him, but Texas is a whole different world."

As we talk, the front bell jingles, and in walks Carson, his face a mix of apprehension and hope. Our gazes meet, and there's a silent understanding that we need to talk, *really talk* this time.

"Let's go to my office," I suggest, leading the way. The small space feels intimate, a haven for the heart-to-heart we so desperately need.

Carson closes the door behind us, the click sounding final, like the start of something crucial. "Naomi, I... I've been thinking all night. I was wrong to spring this on you, to expect you to just upend your life without considering what you want. I didn't realize we hadn't discussed where we'd live until I got back from Texas. It seemed obvious to me, but I should have made sure we were on the same page."

I sit down, the weight of our situation heavy in the air. "I love you, but this diner is a part of me. I've poured everything into it. Leaving it, even partially, feels like leaving part of myself behind."

He moves closer, his eyes earnest. "I get that, I really do, because it's the same for me with my business. I'm sorry I didn't see it before. I just... I want a life with you. I can't imagine being without you."

The vulnerability in his voice tugs at something deep within me. "And I can't imagine being without you either, but I'm not sure how we can make this work."

He takes my hands in his, the contact bridging the gap between us. "What if we try splitting our time? I can be more flexible with my business in Texas. We can make both places our home."

The idea, daunting yet filled with potential, begins to

take shape in my mind. "Split our time?" I echo, the words feeling strange yet hopeful.

"Yes," he says, squeezing my hands. "I love you, Naomi. I want to be with you, wherever that might be. We can find a way to make it work, together."

Tears prick my eyes, a mix of relief and love washing over me. "That could work. We could make it work."

Carson and I face each other, the air thick with the weight of our decisions and the love that has brought us to this crucial moment. "Okay, let's talk logistics," I say, trying to sound more confident than I feel. "If we're going to split our time between Branson and Texas, we need a plan."

Carson nods, his eyes meeting mine. "I agree. I can be in Branson for a few weeks at a time. I'll have to make frequent trips back to Texas, but I can work remotely to some extent."

I chew on my lip, considering his words. "And I can hire a manager for the daily operations to run things here. I think Jenny could step up as manager, which would free me up to be with you."

He reaches across the desk, taking my hands in his. "I don't want you to feel like you're abandoning the diner. It's a big part of who you are."

I squeeze his hands, grateful for his understanding. "I know, but being with you is just as important. We'll make it work, Carson. We have to." "I'm scared," I admit, my voice barely above a whisper. "I've never lived anywhere but Branson. The thought of leaving is daunting, but losing you is something I don't want to contemplate."

He leans closer, his gaze intense. "I understand, and I'm scared too, but I'm also excited about the possibilities of what we can build together."

The idea of a shared future, of building something new and beautiful together, begins to take root in my heart. "We could travel and see new places together. I think I could make a second home in Texas."

Carson's smile is gentle, full of promise. "I love that idea."

As the conversation winds down, a sense of peace settles over us. The doubts and fears that had once seemed insurmountable now feel like challenges we can overcome together.

Standing to leave the office, Carson's hand is in mine, a tangible reminder of the strength of our bond. We step out into the diner, the familiar surroundings a symbol of my past and our future.

We walk through the diner, the place where it all began for us. It's a symbol of my roots, of the community I love, and now, it's also a symbol of our love and the future we're building together.

With Carson by my side, I'm ready to face whatever the future holds, knowing that together, we're stronger.

I take a deep breath, feeling Carson's presence beside me, grounding and reassuring. "This is going to be a big change," I say, my voice a mix of excitement and apprehension. "Not just for me, but for the diner too."

He squeezes my hand, his eyes reflecting understanding and support. "I know, but I believe in you, Naomi. You've built something incredible here, and that's not going to change just because you're not here every day."

I nod, reassured by his confidence in me. "And you're sure you can handle the back-and-forth? Texas isn't exactly a short drive away."

Carson chuckles softly, a sound that warms me from the inside. "I've spent my life traveling for work. A few hours on a plane is nothing compared to being able to find a way to be with you and spend time in this place that's become part of me now."

His words fill me with a surge of love and gratitude. "I can't wait to see Texas through your eyes," I say, envisioning the new experiences awaiting us.

"And I can't wait to show it to you," he says, his gaze full of promise. "We'll explore my hometown, visit Ellen, and maybe even find some new real estate opportunities."

The idea of blending our lives, of creating a shared existence between two places, begins to take shape in my mind. "It sounds exciting. A little scary, but I'm looking forward to it."

As we take a booth in the corner, our conversation turns to more immediate plans. The diner's reopening has been a success, and with Jenny stepping up as manager once I offer her the promotion, I feel more confident about leaving it in capable hands. "We'll need to train Jenny and make sure she's comfortable with everything," I say, already making mental notes.

Carson nods, his business acumen kicking in. "And we'll set up regular check-ins, maybe even some remote management tools. I can help with that."

Noon approaches, bringing an influx of customers. Carson pitches in with delivering orders as we continue talking, planning, and dreaming while passing each other during the lunch rush.

My stomach flutters with nervous excitement as I contemplate the new chapter before us, filled with challenges and uncertainties, but also with endless possibilities. Together, we're embarking on a journey that will take us beyond the familiar streets of Branson, into a future that we'll create side by side.

As the last lunch customer leaves, I stop and look up at Carson. "This is it, isn't it? The start of something new."

He pulls me close, his arms encircling me. "Yes, Naomi. It's just the beginning."

We stand there, our hearts full of hope and love, ready to face whatever the future holds. Together, we are stronger, our bond unbreakable, and our journey just beginning.

27

SEALED WITH A KISS – CARSON

Today, under the brilliant Missouri late spring sky, I'm marrying Naomi. Everything feels surreal, from the vibrant flowers lining the aisle to the gathering of friends and family, all here to witness the union of two souls who found each other against all odds.

I stand at the altar, my heart racing with anticipation. The soft rustle of Naomi's dress announces her arrival, and as she steps into view, my breath catches. She's stunning, a vision in white, her smile radiating the joy that fills my heart. Our eyes meet, and in that moment, everything else fades away.

As Naomi glides down the aisle created by rose petals strewn down a makeshift row in the park, where we're having the wedding, every step she takes is a beat in the symphony of our love story. The light catches in her hair, cascading down her shoulders like a golden waterfall. Her dress, a masterpiece of lace and silk, hugs her in all the right places, making her look like she stepped out of a fairy tale.

Our guests stand from their folding chairs, their faces bright with smiles and a few teary eyes. The scent of the fresh flowers mixes with the late spring air, creating an intoxicating aroma that fills the outdoor space. I can hear the soft whisper of fabric, the gentle sighs of our families and friends, all gathered to celebrate this moment with us.

As Naomi reaches the altar, her older brother gives her hand to mine. Our fingers intertwine, a physical manifestation of our hearts joining together. "You look amazing," I whisper, earning a blushing smile that lights up her face.

The minister begins, his voice steady and warm. We exchange vows, each word soaked in emotion and promise. When I say, "I do," it's more than just a phrase. It's a pledge of my heart, my soul, and my everything to Naomi.

The kiss we share as we are pronounced husband and wife is tender yet full of passion, a seal on our promises to each other. The area erupts in applause and cheers, a joyful sound that echoes our happiness.

We move from the park to the diner for our reception. It's our special place, and the atmosphere is electric. The tables are adorned with white tablecloths and centerpieces of delicate flowers. The air is filled with the sound of chatter, laughter, and clinking glasses.

Naomi and I make our rounds, greeting guests, and thanking them for being part of our day. Each handshake and each hug adds to the tapestry of our joy. "We did it," Naomi whispers to me as we move through the crowd. "We really did."

Our first dance is like floating in a dream. The song is soft and romantic, a melody that speaks of enduring love and devotion. Naomi rests her head on my shoulder, and we sway gently, lost in our world. The warmth of her body against mine is a reminder of the life we're about to build together.

As the night wears on, the makeshift dance floor fills

with guests, the music a lively rhythm that matches the beat of our hearts. We laugh, dance, and celebrate not just our union, but the journey that brought us here.

When the evening winds down, and the last guests depart, Naomi and I stand hand in hand, looking at the now-empty diner. "This is just the beginning," I say, feeling an overwhelming sense of anticipation.

Naomi smiles up at me, her eyes shining with love and happiness. "Yes, it is. Our beginning."

We step outside to find the guests assembled with bird-seed in hand. They shower us with it as we dash to my waiting car. Naomi's younger brother, or maybe my brothers, have decked it out with the gaudiest finery of newly-weds—shaving cream, tin cans, and balloons.

After leaving the lively celebration of our wedding reception, Naomi and I make our way to the small local airport. The excitement of our honeymoon adventure adds an extra spring to our steps. We board a small charter plane, the convenience and speed far outweighing a long drive. Our destination is the serene Smoky Mountains.

As the plane takes off, Naomi's hand finds mine, her grip firm and reassuring. The world below gradually becomes a patchwork of lights and shadows, and I sense the anticipation building between us.

"We're married," she says, her eyes gleaming with excitement. "A new chapter, and just the two of us."

I nod, my heart swelling with joy. "The perfect start to our married life. Just wait until you see the cabin I booked. It's secluded, cozy, and right in the heart of the mountains."

The flight is smooth, and we spend most of it talking about our plans—hiking trails we want to explore, lazy mornings we want to spend in bed, and evenings by the fireplace. The intimacy of the small plane makes it feel like we're in our own little world, soaring toward a dream.

Landing at a small airport near the Smokies, the cool mountain air greets us, refreshing and invigorating. We collect our luggage and head to the car rental desk. After claiming our SUV, we program the GPS. I imagine the drive is scenic in the daylight, but it's dark now, and we can't see much of the lush forests and sparkling streams surrounding us. We'll have plenty of time to explore during our ten days here.

Upon arriving at the cabin, it's everything I promised and more. Nestled among towering pines, it offers privacy and breathtaking views of the surrounding wilderness. Naomi's delight is evident as she steps out of the car, her gaze taking in the beauty of our surroundings.

The cabin itself is a blend of rustic charm and modern comfort. A large stone fireplace dominates the living room, while floor-to-ceiling windows provide panoramic views of the forest. The wooden interior, combined with soft, plush furnishings, creates a welcoming atmosphere.

"We could just stay here forever," she says, a look of pure happiness on her face.

I wrap my arms around her, sharing her sentiment. "As long as I'm with you, I'm home."

We're both exhausted from the wedding and hours of traveling, so we cook a simple but delicious meal together, the kitchen proving to be well-stocked and user-friendly. We dine by candlelight, the ambiance of the cabin adding a romantic touch to our first meal as a married couple.

After dinner, we retire to the living room, the fire crackling in the hearth. We talk, laugh, and reminisce, the fire's warm glow enveloping us in its embrace. It's a perfect, peaceful end to an eventful day.

As she yawns repeatedly, and so do I, we decide to move from the living room to the bedroom. We make our way to the bedroom, the softness of the bed a welcome comfort. Naomi curls up against me, her warmth a soothing presence. In the quiet of the mountain night, with my wife in my arms, I feel a profound sense of contentment.

"I love you, Naomi," I whisper, my heart full.

"I love you too, Carson," she replies, her voice soft and loving. "I'll show you just how much in the morning."

I laugh. "I'm looking forward to it." We're both too exhausted right now to make love and do it justice. I let my eyes close and savor having her against me. Drifting off to sleep, I think about our future, about the adventures and challenges we'll face together, but for now, in our secluded mountain retreat, everything is perfect.

Epilogue – Naomi

Three Years Later

Eli bounces in his booster seat beside me in the limo. "I wanna see my aunties and Uncle Luke and Uncle Wyatt and Uncle Raylan."

I pat his leg. "You will. We'll be in Branson for a while. I want to see all the family, but first, we need to settle in our condo, and you could use a nap."

My toddler glares at me and then at his father. "I'm not sleepy." With that defiant pronouncement, he yawns.

Carson chuckles. "Clearly not."

"No nap," he says, crossing his arms.

"We'll see about that," I say, knowing that a few blocks of driving will put him to sleep.

Carson kisses the top of his head. "Be good for Mommy, okay?"

"Okay, Daddy. Love you." He bats his thick dark lashes at Carson, and he visibly melts.

"Maybe you don't need a nap today."

I give him a shake of my head. "Don't make me the bad guy, you big softie."

He grins at me. "Wouldn't dream of it, dear."

"Sure, you wouldn't." I scoff but quickly kiss him before turning back to Eli. "If you're still awake when we get to our condo, you won't have to take a nap."

He's already blinking. "Good. I don't need one." He yawns.

"Of course not," says Carson as he leans back in his seat.

I snuggle into his side, and he wraps his arm around me. As the limo pulls away from the airport, I sigh with contentment. "It's good to be back in Branson." Texas has grown on me the past three years, but Branson is still the home of my heart, and I always feel a little more content when we're staying here.

"It is." Carson squeezes my hand. "I know how much you love it here, so I thought we'd spend some extra time this trip. We'll stay a whole month instead of just a week. That way, we can really enjoy the time with your family and our friends. I thought you'd want to stay longer anyway. At least long enough for Allegra to give birth. Luke says she's about to pop."

"That sounds perfect." I smile up at him. "I'm sure Eli will be thrilled to play with his cousins. He loves spending time with Ellen, but there aren't any young kids in your family in Texas."

He sighs. "I know."

It seems like the perfect time to tell him. I sneak a peek at Eli, whose head is tipped against his padded belt. He's snoring quietly despite resisting his nap for all he's worth. "I guess we'll just have to make sure he has playmates in Texas too."

"Are you thinking about preschool?" Carson's eyes widen. "That's a bit far off, isn't it?"

"Hmm, not really. Three or four is typical for preschool, and I think he'd like going a couple of mornings per week, but I was thinking more along the lines of siblings."

His jaw drops. "Siblings? You mean more children?"

I nod.

He shakes his head. "I don't know if I'm ready for that. I still haven't forgotten the delivery."

I smack him lightly on the arm. "When you're the one going through birth, then you can complain."

Carson smiles. "I meant your pain. I hated seeing you hurting."

"It was worth it." I lean in closer to him. "Do you remember that amazing night in the hot tub six weeks ago?"

His eyes gleam. "When Ellen had Eli overnight... Yes. Are you thinking of recreating it at the condo?" Desire sparks in his gaze.

"Sadly, no. The water is too hot for a while. Do you remember what happened that night...what we forgot?"

He frowns. "I didn't forget anything."

I grin. "Really? Nothing?"

"Nothing." His brow furrows deeper. "What did I forget?"

"We forgot something that night." I bite my lip. "Something important. Something we've been using for the past three years..."

His eyes widen as he remembers. "The condom." Then his gaze narrows as he obviously puts it all together. "You're pregnant?"

I nod. "Yes. I took the test this morning."

He blinks rapidly. "How far along?"

"About six weeks." I laugh at him. "We just established that."

He blushes but laughs. "I guess my brain is scrambled." A smile spreads across his face. "Another baby. Wow."

I nod. "I know. I'm as shocked as you are. I thought it was stress from getting ready for the Branson trip until I realized we forgot something that night, so I took a test."

"And it was positive?"

"Yep. I'm definitely pregnant."

Carson's eyes shine with happiness. "This is incredible. I can't wait to tell everyone."

I put my hand on his arm. "Let's keep it quiet for now. We don't want to steal the spotlight from Luke and Allegra. Let's wait until after their baby is born."

He nods. "That makes sense. It's just hard not to share the news with everyone. This is a big deal, Naomi. We're going to be parents again."

"I know." I smile at him. "Trust me, I'm just as excited as you are, but we can wait a few weeks to tell everyone. It's not like we're going to forget we're pregnant in that amount of time."

He laughs. "No, I suppose not." His expression turns serious. "Do you think Eli will be happy?"

"Yes. Probably a little jealous, but I think, overall, he's going to be a great big brother and happy to have a sibling."

"Me too." Carson kisses the top of my head as the limo pulls up to the condo in a row of townhouses we own here in Branson. It made more sense to buy a place of our own, and Jenny took over my apartment when she became manager of the diner, so she could be close to work.

"Home sweet home," I say as I step out of the limo and stretch.

Carson carries Eli inside without waking him as the driver brings our bags. The housekeeper has already stocked the fridge and pantry, so we can relax and enjoy the rest of the day.

I follow behind, smiling at the sight of my husband carrying our son. I can easily picture him with two kids in his arms, and I'm excited for the future, and to meet the little one growing inside me.

Eli stirs as Carson lays him on the bed. "Mommy?"

"Hi, sweetheart. We're here."

He rubs his eyes. "Where's here?"

"Our condo in Branson. Remember, we're going to stay for a while?"

He nods. "Right." His eyes are already drifting closed again, and he grasps my forefinger as he goes back to sleep.

I smile down at him and then turn to Carson, who's watching us with a tender expression. "It's nice to be home."

"It is." He wraps his arm around me, pulling me closer. "Texas will always be my home, but Branson has grown on me."

"I feel the same, but in reverse." I snuggled closer. "Truthfully, wherever you are is home to me."

He leans in and kisses me softly. "Same."

I smile at him. "You know, Eli won't wake for at least an hour..." I wiggle my eyebrows. "Want to take advantage of our alone time?"

Carson grins and lifts me into his arms. "Always." He carries me into the bedroom, where he proceeds to make love to me slowly and passionately, drawing out every ounce of pleasure from our bodies.

Afterward, we lie together, sated and content, enjoying the closeness of each other's embrace. I nestle closer to Carson, breathing in his familiar scent. There's nowhere else I'd rather be than right here, in his arms, with our son sleeping soundly in the next room. We've come a long way since that first meeting in the diner, and I wouldn't change a thing about our journey together.

I sigh happily as Carson kisses my cheek. "I love you, Naomi," he whispers.

"I love you too, Carson." And I do, with all my heart.

<u>**The Billionaire Branson Brothers Collection:**</u>

- Wyatt: A Small Town, Opposites Attract Romance
- Luke: A Small Town, Secret Pregnancy Romance
- Jesse: A Small Town, Second Chance Romance
- Raylan: A Small Town, Fake Fiance Romance
- Carson: A Small Town, Secret Son, Billionaire Romance

<u>**The Unlikely Billionaire Collection:**</u>

- Hard at Work With My Best Friend's Grumpy Twin
- Broken Down With the Secret Billionaire

Join Lexi's Lovers Newsletter to stay up to date on all of Lexi's new releases, special giveaways, and book recommendations from other great authors!

If you enjoyed Carson and Naomi's love story, read on for a sneak

peek at The Billionaire Branson Brothers: Raylan. Coming July 23, 2024 to online retailers.

The winding, hilly Missouri roads are a little difficult to navigate while I'm also trying to find my way to the nature park where I'll be working, but I can already tell I'm going to love my new home—and that peaceful feeling stays with me until I reach a red light and hear the sound of screeching tires. I feel my whole car jolt forward, and I don't even have time to scream, but a startled gasp escapes my throat as my brain tries to process what the heck just happened.

I look up to see a dark truck idling behind me. One of its headlights looks smashed up from where it hit me, and I can only imagine what the rear end of my car looks like. My heart's already racing, and a surge of adrenaline pulses through me. My car is still moving, and I press the brake and shift into neutral before I throw the car into park.

I open the door and jump out, rushing toward the car's rear. I hope the other driver is okay and there isn't too much damage to my car. This is my first day in a new town, on my way to a new job, and I need wheels.

I sure can't afford any unexpected expenses right now.

The truck door opens, and the first thing I notice about the other driver is that he's big—muscular and tall, definitely over six feet.

The next thing I notice is the surly frown on his face.

He looks like he should be in some kind of magazine for rugged outdoorsmen. *Angry* rugged outdoorsmen.

My mouth goes dry, and I can't help but stare.

But as soon as he walks toward me, his shoulders rigid and his fists clenched, I feel a knot of worry form in my gut. He doesn't look happy, and I consider jumping back in my car and locking the doors.

But before I can move, he's towering over me.

"Are you okay?" he asks, his tone rough and gravelly as he gives me a quick up-and-down look.

"Yeah." I nod, swallowing hard and giving myself a quick mental once-over. I'm so hyped up on adrenaline that it might take a few hours before I know if I will be sore, bruised, or worse, but I'm okay for now. "I—I think so. But —"

"Then what the hell were you doing?" he interrupts, any inkling of concern he might have had in his voice vanishing in an instant. "The light turned green, and you were just sitting there. You're damn lucky I wasn't going any faster."

Um, *what*? I can't believe the nerve of this guy.

My mouth opens and closes several times as a surge of indignant anger rushes through me. "I'm *lucky*? I'm pretty sure you're the one who ran into me."

I point behind us to my car and the mess of plastic and metal that used to be a headlight on his truck.

"You're seriously blaming me?" He laughs bitterly and shakes his head, his eyes raking me up and down again, making me feel like he's undressing me with his gaze. "It's gawking tourists like you who get people killed on the roads around here every damn day."

My jaw drops, and I can't believe this jerk. "I'm not a tourist, thank you very much," I scoff, shooting him a dirty look. "And I wasn't gawking. I'm on my way to work, and now you've just guaranteed I'll be late on my first day, so thanks a lot for that."

To my surprise, his stern, stony expression softens a little. But only a little, and it's such a subtle change that I probably would've missed it if I weren't staring so intensely at his grumpy face.

His handsome, grumpy face with that movie-star jawline

and eyes are so blue that it feels like he's looking into my soul.

"You're local?"

"Well, not exactly," I admit. "But I just moved here. Like, the day before yesterday."

He shakes his head, his lips pressing together, his eyes narrowing at me.

And then, without another word, he walks past me and stops behind my car, his eyes scanning the back bumper of my car. "Doesn't look as bad as I thought it would be. Again, lucky for you."

I want to say something scathing—or at least sarcastic—but I've got nothing. I'm still too rattled by the accident and his complete, unapologetic rudeness.

"If your insurance information is in your car, I can call it in, and we can both be on our way," he says.

It takes me a second to realize that he's talking to me.

"I'm sorry, what?" I ask, blinking a few times and hoping he can't tell that I've been staring at him.

He sighs and looks up at the sky for a moment, and I get the feeling that he's trying hard not to lose his patience with me.

Which, because he's the one who rear-ended me, is not a fair reaction.

"Look," he says, his voice taking on a much more reasonable tone. "I'd like to just go on my way, but we need to call the cops and get a report so we can exchange insurance information and figure out how to fix this."

He points at my bumper, and I can see that his truck has pushed it in a little, but the damage is minimal.

I'd be lying if I said I wasn't relieved.

"There's no way your insurance will cover it if we don't have a police report," he adds, those blue eyes making my stomach flip despite myself. He's a total jerk, but he's also a real hunk, and my body seems to have a mind of its own when it comes to men.

Especially angry, handsome, grumpy men.

"Uh...okay," I stammer. "Yeah. I have my insurance in my glove box. Just let me grab it."

"Great."

I rush back over to my car, my face burning. I can feel him watching me, and my skin tingles a little with every second his eyes linger.

What is wrong with me? Why am I reacting to him like this?

I grab my paperwork and get back out of the car. The air is cooler, but the sun is warm and feels good on my flushed face.

"Here you go," I say, handing him my insurance verification. "I'm Cassidy, by the way. Cassidy Turner."

"Nice to meet you," he says, not bothering to give me his name in return.

He takes his phone out of his pocket and holds it up. "Okay, well, if you don't mind, Cassidy, I'll call the cops and thee a quick picture of this so we have documentation. I've got an early meeting and will already be late. I can't spend all day dealing with this."

Again, the audacity.

"Fine," I shrug, not even trying to hide the exasperation in my tone.

His eyes lock with mine, and they sparkle a little momentarily, almost like he's fighting a smile. That can't be right, though. This guy looks like he hasn't smiled in years.

Once he's made the phone call to the cops and we've exchanged information, I head back to my battered car and watch in my rearview mirror while he climbs back into his shiny black truck.

Yeah, he's hot. But damn, what a jerk.

I'll be just fine if I never see his handsome face again.

Keep reading Raylan and Cassidy's story at online retailers.